Caribe

Maria Urbina-Fauser

Tellwell Talent
www.tellwell.ca

ISBN
978-0-2288-8096-7 (Paperback)
978-0-2288-8097-4 (eBook)

To Simón and Mateo, from the bottom of the sea...

Para Daniela,
con cariño
María

ONE

Shipwreck

THE NIGHT OF SEPTEMBER 3RD, 2007 was not a good one for the sailboat *Las Luces*. She was cruising through the Caribbean Sea, south of Jamaica, after having set sail three days earlier from Vela de Coro, Venezuela. The vessel was headed to Turks and Caicos, and was crewed by a Venezuelan family, seven-year-old twins Alba and Tiago and their mother Cecilia. The Castillos were a very special family. Cecilia and her husband had built the sailboat and had lived on it for almost five years before Alba and Tiago were born. Her husband passed away before meeting the twins, so she had to raise them alone in the sea, with the help of her own mom, Coromoto.

Cecilia was a marine archaeologist and an experienced sailor who knew the Caribbean sea from end to end. She had been invited to an underwater archaeological exploration to look for a sunken brig believed to be the *Trouvadore*, which was one of thousands of slave ships that transported more than ten million African slaves from West Africa to the Americas, between the years 1525 and 1866. What made the *Trouvadore* extraordinary was that when it sank in the Caribbean in 1841, it freed 192 African passengers otherwise destined for slavery. This exploration of the *Trouvadore* would be the culmination of three years of study, in which she hoped to find some connection between the slaves freed in the shipwreck and her own ancestors.

Although they were small, Alba and Tiago gave indications that they too would follow in their mother's footsteps. Alba could easily read the sea and the waves, and Tiago felt a complete fascination for the stars which he knew by heart. The two children helped their mother navigate; and they did so just as well as any more experienced crew.

But that night in September, not even the best sailors stood a chance. The great tropical hurricane Felix hit the Caribbean, leaving hundreds of victims in its wake, including the Castillo family and their boat.

TWO

Tiago

TIAGO WAS TALL FOR FOURTEEN, and people always assumed he was older. He had dark skin, big cocoa eyes, and shaggy brown hair that turned golden in the summer. He was easy-going and people enjoyed being around him. Tiago lived in a small town on Vancouver Island, Canada, where his dad taught at the local college and his mom owned a bookstore.

His parents called him Tiggy; only they weren't his birth parents. Tiago's mother and his twin sister Alba had drowned at sea eight years earlier and Tiago was found perched like a small seagull on what remained of the sinking boat's mast. He was dehydrated and bruised, but otherwise unharmed. By luck, the Curaçao Coastal Guard had been patrolling the area, well north of its jurisdiction. They brought him to Willemstad where they kept him at *Sint Elisabeth Hospital*. They asked him lots of questions, such as how had he managed to climb up the broken mast; but he had no idea. The search for his family was abandoned after a few weeks and Tiago would have been sent to the city's orphanage had he not met Perry and Margaret Tremblay, a Canadian couple volunteering at the hospital.

Tiago didn't remember much of his time in the hospital, but he knew he felt alone and was filled with uncertainty and a terrible sadness. The kindness and love of his adoptive parents helped him slowly heal, but he never stopped wanting to know what had really happened that night. Even eight years later, he continued to think about the hurricane and read anything he could find on it. As soon as he was old enough, he planned to go back to the Caribbean, to the exact coordinates 16°46'N 76°40'W, where he had lost his family.

Tiago's mother tongue was Spanish and he made sure he didn't forget it, taking it as a class in high school and attending Spanish school on Saturday mornings. He read every Spanish language book he could find and listened to the Venezuelan radio.

His adoptive parents took him to Venezuela in 2010 when he was ten years old, to help him try and find members of his extended family. The country and its people were already suffering the negative effects of the government's misguided economic policies. Poverty, shortage of food, electricity blackouts, and an overall air of disenchantment with president Chávez prevailed.

Finding Tiago's remaining relatives proved to be very difficult; none of the Castillos they met were related to him and he couldn't recall any other last names. He remembered his grandma, *Abuela Moto*, vividly and he missed her as much as his mother and sister. Unfortunately, he couldn't remember any useful details that could help locate her, only that she had lived on Margarita Island. After some time searching, they assumed she had passed away.

One day in September, 2015, exactly eight years after the wreckage, Tiago received a document in the mail. He had been tracking down the historical records of the Puerto Cabello Coast Guard for the year 2007 and they had finally arrived. Excited, he quickly turned to September where he discovered the following entry in Spanish:

"September 16, 3:47pm, telegram from Aguide advising arrival on shore the day before (September 15), 11:39am of a girl of six or seven years of age, named Alba Castillo, health stable, claimed to be a survivor of a shipwrecked, sailboat Las Luces, on the way to Turks and Caicos."

Tiago's head spun with hundreds of questions, but his heart was full of certainty. Alba was alive and most likely in Venezuela. In that moment he knew exactly what he had to do – he would go to find her.

Alba

ALBA WAS FOURTEEN YEARS OLD and she had lived her entire life in the Caribbean. Her eyes had never stopped seeing a blue horizon and her body had not gone a day without swimming in the salty water. Even after the shipwreck, she could not get away from the sea.

Alba was able to escape Hurricane Felix eight years earlier. When she arrived on the shores of a small Venezuelan town called Aguide, thirteen days after the boat sank, no one could understand how she had survived. She was exhausted, starving, and scared, but otherwise healthy. Alba remembered her grandmother Moto's last name: Flores. *Doña Coromoto* lived on the island of Margarita and the authorities were able to contact her. Two days later, Coromoto arrived in Aguide, hugged her granddaughter and took her back to the island.

Alba was small and strong, dark skinned with untamed brown hair, full of curls and knots. She had large brown eyes and was almost always barefoot, unless her grandmother made her put on shoes. She preferred the company of nature to that of humans, and every day she spent hours swimming in the sea. Alba felt uncomfortable on dry land, having to act a certain way around people. She had no close friends, and felt raw anger every time she got a look of pity from her neighbours.

Alba had lived in Boca de Pozo since she was seven years old. It was a small fishing village on the Macanao Peninsula, on the western end of Margarita island. There the passage of life was marked by the tide and the wind, by the departure of the fishing boats at sunset, and their arrival at dawn. Life had become more and more difficult for the inhabitants of Boca de Pozo. Every year the number of fishermen who died at sea, victims of pirates, increased; and those who did return had smaller catches. There were also more smugglers trafficking gasoline and other goods, making the sea that Alba loved so much incredibly dangerous.

At her school, she learned about the rest of the world, about big and important cities, and about different customs in other countries, but she did not have much interest in the outside world. What she wanted was to improve things in her own country. She wanted to study and find a way to help fishing villages like Boca de Pozo.

FOUR

Tiago

T IAGO LOCKED HIMSELF IN his dad's office as soon as he got home from school and began to plan his next move. He googled everything he could find about the best way to get to Aguide, Estado Falcón, Venezuela – which was the last place he knew Alba had been.

Tiago could have told his parents the news. It would have been easy, and they would have supported him and helped him make his way to Aguide. However, he had a feeling they would not find much in that town, and it would take more digging to get any real clues to his sister's whereabouts. He knew his parents, and he was certain they would give up after a short while, especially considering Venezuela was not the safest of countries. Tiago realized he had to go alone, and he would have to dedicate himself to the adventure. He couldn't ask his parents to do the same, and he knew they wouldn't anyway.

After a few hours, Tiago had his plan. He would ask his parents if he could visit his adoptive grandparents in Florida for Thanksgiving, in mid-October. Every year, he visited them on his own, travelling by plane as an unaccompanied minor to West Palm Beach, where they would spend a week together swimming, telling stories, playing board games, and eating ice cream. Tiago loved his vacations with his grandparents, but this one would be very different. He planned to sneak away, leaving them a letter explaining everything. He would join a sailing crew travelling to the Caribbean and work as a deckhand to get as close as possible to Venezuela. The details of the latter part of his plan weren't yet clear in his mind, but he accepted he would have to wing it. First, he needed money, so he decided to sell his most prized possession, his *Laser 4.7*, a small sailing dinghy he took out every weekend.

The weeks flew by and soon he was making the solo trip from Vancouver Island to Palm Beach. Tiago's parents drove him to the Victoria airport and said their farewells. He didn't know if he'd ever see them again, and suddenly the thought of truly spending the week at his grandparents and then coming back home didn't seem so bad at all. He hugged them fiercely and let all the gratitude in the world wash over him. He shouldn't abandon them now. He could always go find his sister another time when things were better in Venezuela; maybe even when he was an adult… when he wasn't scared, when he didn't need his parents, when he wouldn't worry about things like being able to handle the simple plane transfer in Toronto on his own. He pushed these thoughts aside and decided to focus on getting to his grandparents. He pulled away from his mom and dad and showed them with a big smile just how much he loved them.

The trip was uneventful, and in time Tiago found himself in another hug, this time with his grandparents. He was happy to see them, but also felt guilty about the worry he would put them through if he went ahead with his crazy plan.

FIVE

Alba

Doña Coromoto sensed something was weighing heavy on Alba's mind. One afternoon she found her alone in deep contemplation at her favorite beach, staring out at the quiet sea. *Abuela Moto* sat next to her with some effort:

"Albita, what are you thinking my girl? I can see you're worried," She said, grunting as she sat down.

"Oh, Grandma!" Alba sighed. "What can I tell you? Have you ever had to do something really hard and you didn't know how to do it?"

"Yes."

"And how did you do it?"

"The trick is not to think about it too much. The more you think about it, the more it eats away at you. You just have to take the first step and everything else follows."

"Well, that's it then." Alba sounded resigned.

"Is it something I can help you with?" *Abuela Moto* asked. "No, grandmother, it's something I have to do by myself." "Well, that's it then… As you say."

"Aren't you going to ask me what it is?" Alba sounded surprised.

"No, if you want to tell me, you'll tell me. And if you don't, then it's not worth asking." "Well, I do want to tell you but I'm afraid you won't let me do it."

"From what I can see," said *Abuela Moto*, looking sweetly at her granddaughter. "This is serious and I don't think I have the power to decide for you."

So Alba opened her mouth and her heart and explained to her grandmother that she was sure that Tiago was alive, living in Canada, and that she was going to look for him. *Abuela Moto* listened with surprise, cried a long time, and then laughed with much joy. She never doubted, as other adults would, her granddaughter's words. She knew in her heart that it was all true, and she also knew that Alba had to go find Tiago, and she had to do it by sea. *Abuela Moto* understood that with the internet and phones they could easily locate Tiago, without the girl having to go off on a dangerous adventure. But *Abuela Moto* had a secret of her own and this was the time to share it with Alba. She had kept this secret all of her long life, only telling her own daughter, Alba's mother, many years ago.

"Alba, I also have something to tell you," *Doña Coromoto* hesitated. "The thing is, I can't find the words…" She was silent for a long time and Alba had to wait and wait until, at last, *Coromoto* slowly stood up from the sand and whispered, "It might be better if I show you."

Abuela Moto opened the palm of her right hand, turning it towards the sky, and moved it from her right side to her left and back, in a kind of slow dance. Immediately a breeze from the west, strong but pleasant, caressed the surface of the sea cutting a path through the waves and forming a channel. Alba looked at her grandmother in disbelief. She understood perfectly that the slight wind was moving the sea and that her grandmother somehow moved the air, but she didn't understand how she was doing it. *Doña Coromoto* winked at her and made a fist, and the wind grew stronger and began to swirl in a whirlpool, raising the water into a spiral as it grew to form a huge funnel-shaped tower. With a final gesture, *Abuela Moto* opened her hand, and the whirlwind of sea collapsed, creating a huge wave which soaked them both, and blowing a wind that left Alba's hair with many more knots than it already had.

SIX

Tiago

TIAGO'S GRANDPARENTS' CONDO WAS a short walk to a number of marinas. On the first morning he decided to visit the closest one. Tiago was still unsure if he would go through with his plan, but he decided to scope out some of the vessels preparing to leave.

Having spent his first seven years on a boat, Tiago was an avid sailor and had continued to sail in Canada, encouraged by his parents who knew it was a big part of who he was. They thought he loved the sea, but Tiago truly, more than anything, loved the sky and the wind, and that's why he sailed. Reading the wind, the clouds, and at night – the stars, was like solving a math puzzle with both his brain and his instincts. And the boat would always tell him if he didn't get it right. If wrong, he corrected course and trimmed the sails until he got it perfect. Tiago loved the certainty of knowing there was always a correct answer and a way to keep going forward.

At the marina, he watched the crew of a twenty-metre racing yacht prepare the vessel. Eight sailors went to and fro packing provisions, checking lines, and testing equipment, and every single one of them wore excited smiles. Even with his doubts, Tiago felt the pull of adventure. Maybe he *should* go.

On his second to last day in Florida, Tiago still had not made up his mind. He needed to decide soon because he was running out of time. He had been to five marinas and didn't know what he was searching for. He would just stand and watch the crews for hours, and then go back to spend time with his grandparents. That morning, he got up early and went to a marina in South Palm Beach. He was eating a bagel watching a couple on their boat and couldn't help but chuckle as they tried to dock the tiny four-metre vessel. They kept losing their position because they didn't account for the easterly wind pushing them away from the pier. As the man's hat went flying, Tiago looked up and spotted it... *Hope*; the most beautiful sailboat he'd ever seen. It was around fourteen metres long and painted bright yellow, including the mast and boom, which were gold anodized. The white sails were furled as it approached slowly by motor. The captain was at the helm – a handsome young man with a mop of blond hair almost as yellow as his boat, wearing huge polarized sunglasses, and an orange jacket. The whole picture made Tiago think of sunshine and orange juice, and the Beatles' song *Yellow Submarine*. It was almost too much, like staring at the sun for too long, but he was enthralled.

He followed the boat to its dock and offered the young skipper a hand with the ropes.

"Hi, she's a beautiful boat. Need help?"

"Yeah, thanks. That'd be swell Little Bird!" answered the young captain. He spoke with a high-pitched ringing voice, almost as if he were singing, and he had a long, slow drawl when he said the word *swell* that automatically made Tiago smile. They tied in quickly.

"So, what's your name?"

"Tiggy… I mean, Tiago," he corrected himself. "Nice to meet you."

"I'm Sandy. Sandy Shores, with an S," he said, "For surf, sail, and sunshine!"

All those S's made Tiago's head spin. "Your name is Sandy Shores? For real?"

"Totes my friend, totes! Alexander for long, but that's too boring. Sandy it is!" After producing a huge yawn, he continued. "Wanna grab a coffee?"

"I don't drink coffee," Tiago hesitated. "I mean, I'll have orange juice."

"Swell choice, Little Bird. Let's go." Sandy said as he jumped down to the dock.

"Thanks… but do you mind not calling me that anymore? Please?"

"Sure, Little B, you got it."

SEVEN

Alba

S o, what do you think? –asked *Abuela Moto*, looking at her granddaughter's stunned expression.

"I don't understand anything, grandma. Are you a magician? Are you a goddess? Are you even my grandmother? How did you do it? How did you move the wind? Why didn't you tell me? Have you always…"

"Okay, my girl," *Abuela Moto* interrupted. "I will answer everything starting with the fact that yes, I am definitely your grandmother. I am neither a magician nor a goddess. I am Marena."

Abuela Moto shared her story:

"Hundreds of years ago, in the oceans and seas around the world, there was a race that cared for and protected marine life. They were called Marenos or Marinos, depending on the region in which they lived. They had a special affinity with the sea and its elements and they each had something else. All Marenos possessed a special ability, also called a 'gift from the sea.' Some could control the winds, others the waters or the sand, some commanded thunder and lightning, and some Marenos could fly like birds. The most common gift of our lineage was to breathe, swim, and

live in the water like fish, since at some point all the Marenos lived underwater. Little by little they came out to live secretly in small villages on the shore. They helped marine animals, cared for the corals, and maintained the natural balance of the oceans. But with the advances of humanity, the modernization of the fishing industry, pollution, and the disappearance of marine species, the slow extinction of the Marenos has also come. The villages have been dispersed and with each generation fewer Marenos are born. Now, I'm not sure, but there must be no more than a few dozen in the whole world. In the Caribbean there is only one Mareno line left, mine."

"My mother?" Asked Alba.

"Yes, my daughter was Marena too."

"What was her gift?" Alba asked, yet didn't really want to know the answer.

"She could control water…" Her grandmother answered sadly. "That is not possible."

"I understand."

"No, you don't understand Grandma. How could she have controlled the sea if we were shipwrecked in that storm?" Alba exploded in quick anger.

"That's what I understand Albita, your question." *Abuela Moto* sighed with even more sadness. "I understand you because I ask myself the same thing. I ask myself every day."

EIGHT

Tiago

FOUR COFFEES, THREE ORANGE JUICES, and two hours later, Tiago and Sandy were fast friends. It's an understatement that Sandy was a character, with his bleached hair and surfer talk, but Tiago quickly realized that under the airy act there was substance, and he liked him. Sandy was from Key West, a sailor, and expert on all-things-sea from a very young age. He was only seventeen years old, but his fake ID said he was twenty-two. He left home to pursue his dream of sailing around the world in his grandfather's boat, which he had refurbished with his father over the past five years.

Tiago called his grandparents to let them know he'd be home late, and braced himself to share his secret with this perfect stranger. Sandy listened without interrupting or asking any questions. When he finally spoke, he surprised Tiago with his response.

"Dude, you seem so hesitant, like you have a big decision to make, or a choice in the matter. But let me tell you bro, you don't. You just don't. You love your sister. You know she's alive, but you don't know if she is safe. Little Bird, you have to go. This isn't an adventure or a rite of passage; this is the *right* thing to do."

"Right…" said Tiago feeling dumbfounded. All this time he had been thinking about himself, *his* fears, *his* readiness, *his* intentions. But he had forgotten about *her*. Sandy was one hundred percent correct. How could he have been so selfish?

"The good news, bud, is that you've got *me* now. I've recently decided, exactly fifteen seconds ago, to head down to the Caribbean. And I could use some help, I've been single-handing for too long… not sure I'm brave enough to go all the way to Venezuela, but I'll get you as far as I can."

"Right…" said Tiago again, even more stunned. And just like that Tiago's mind was made up; almost for him.

They studied the weather and noticed a favourable window to cross the Gulf Stream; the warm and swift current on the Atlantic Ocean that flows northward along the eastern North American coastline. The stream needed to be traversed in order to reach the Caribbean, but this passage had to be made in perfect weather conditions with no counterwind, or it could be disastrous. It had been forty-eight hours with no wind from the north and barely any from the other directions. A few other boats had been waiting around three weeks to cross and were leaving that night, so Sandy and Tiago decided to join them. They planned to meet at the marina at midnight. Tiago would return to his grandparents and Sandy would prepare the boat and secure food, water, and other supplies.

"But first things first," announced Sandy, calling to the waiter, "Another coffee bro?"

NINE

Alba

S EVERAL DAYS AFTER the conversation with her grandmother, Alba felt totally powerless. She had more questions than she had before and it weighed on her guts that she did not understand why her mother had allowed herself to drown. But the most difficult thing to accept was the last thing her grandmother had said to her. *"You are also Marena and I am sure that your gift is swimming and breathing underwater."* It was the only explanation that *Abuela Moto* could find to justify Alba's arrival eight years ago, on a beach, alone, without a boat or lifeguard, two weeks after the shipwreck.

After that revelation Alba had not bathed in the sea; it was the first time in her fourteen years that she had gone more than a day without swimming. She couldn't face this supposed ability. *Abuela Moto* had explained that perhaps it was latent, since although Alba's gift appeared in a moment of survival, the trauma of the shipwreck probably repressed it again. Alba didn't know what to think and decided to stay out of the sea for now.

Abuela Moto knew how difficult the whole situation was for her granddaughter. She remembered when her own gift was triggered after the death of her mother. Her reality was shaken like a tree in a storm, and although all the leaves in this proverbial tree had fallen, an air of hope lifted them up and caused them to flutter in an encouraging dance. *Doña Coromoto* did not recognize this joy in Alba, only sadness at remembering the shipwreck again, anxiety about her upcoming mission, and anger with her mother and with the sea.

Abuela Moto decided to help her granddaughter in the task of finding her grandson, the only thing that seemed to lift Alba's spirits. She traded her most precious possession: her wedding ring, a memory of her great love, *Don Luis*. She exchanged it for a *peñero*, a wooden fishing boat, typical of the area. It was called *El Guácharo*. The seller explained it had belonged to his father, an explorer of the *Guácharo* Cave in Monagas State, and a lover of the small birds that bear this name. The *peñero* was light brown, painted with small white triangles and wings on each side. *Abuela Moto* thought it was the cutest little boat she had ever seen and a good omen for her granddaughter's journey. The man, seeing *Doña Coromoto's* appreciation for the *peñero*, decided to throw in an old thirty-horsepower motor he had recently repaired. This was an example of the generous acts that *Doña Coromoto* inspired with her smile.

TEN

Tiago

T IAGO RETURNED TO HIS GRANDPARENTS' home. They cooked a lovely meal together and enjoyed a nice and fun dinner. Hugging good night, Tiago thanked them for everything and felt a familiar knot in his throat. He missed them already and felt remorse for what he was about to do.

He went to his room and continued his normal routine, brushing his teeth, and putting on his pajamas before writing a long letter explaining everything. When all was quiet, he tiptoed across the hall to check if they had gone to bed yet. After hearing the usual snoring emanating from their room he packed his backpack, got dressed, and tidied his room. He placed the letter on the kitchen counter and said a silent goodbye as he tried to open the front door. It was locked. He looked around for the keys and realized they must be in his grandparents' room.

He took off his backpack and walked as quietly as possible towards the room. He started to turn the door knob until he saw that this door, too, was locked. '*These two are seriously paranoid,*' he thought, trying not to despair. He wondered for a second if they had suspected his plans, but he remembered his grandpa had always been like that, locking every door he could get his hands on.

He called Sandy, whose first question was how high was the apartment. They were on the third floor of the building and the balcony overlooked the beautifully groomed, sloping gardens of the retirement community. Tiago studied the possibility of climbing down but there was nothing to hang onto. He sat down and accepted his fate to leave in the morning; the Gulf crossing would have to wait until who knew when. But as he looked out from the balcony he felt a tingling sensation, a mix of nerves and happiness. When he was younger, having just moved to Canada, he loved climbing and jumping; he would climb up anything: trees, rocks, buildings, and then jump down. He always felt that very same electric feeling right before jumping, and for a long time he lived for that sensation, which seemed to pierce his sadness and make him feel invincible.

Without thinking, he stood up, strapped his backpack on tight, ran across the living room, leapt off the balcony, and dropped with flailing arms and legs in a slow-motion arch onto the sloped lawn. Right before landing he curled his body and rolled down the grassy knoll unharmed and ecstatic.

ELEVEN

Alba

A T DAWN, *El Guácharo* was anchored near the beach, ready to go. Inside, lay the provisions for the trip: twenty *arepas*, six cans of *diablito* and six of tuna, cookies, some fruits for the first days and many liters of water. There were also two tanks filled with gasoline, one of oil, and a small blue backpack with clothes, a sweater, a blanket, a waterproof compass, a cap, one-hundred American dollars donated by her grandmother, and Alba's most beloved possession, a photo of the three Castillos on their sailboat, kept in a small zip-lock bag.

Alba didn't know what she felt more intensely: determination or fear. It seemed like two forces within her balanced equally, that kept her completely calm as she walked down the beach toward the rock. Determination pushed her forward, facing the unknown. Fear kept her centered. When her feet touched the sea, she felt a small electric current that rose through her body and she knew it was time to say goodbye to her grandmother. She hugged her grandma as tightly as a wave, enveloping her impetuously. Poor *Abuela Moto* needed a few days to recover from the onslaught of love from her grandkid. Saying goodbye to her only reference, her guide, her anchor, Alba suddenly felt despair, which for a moment dissolved all her determination and left only paralyzing fear. *—You will not be alone —*her grandmother whispered, and only these words got Alba to move.

Alba came off the hug abruptly and without looking back she walked into the water, wading to reach the boat. She climbed it with surprising agility, pulled up the anchor and started the engine. Turning around, she looked toward the shore at the little old lady who lost her mother, her husband, then her daughter, and who was now losing her granddaughter. Alba realized she was saying good-bye to the bravest woman in the world.

TWELVE

Tiago

"**N**O WAY YOU JUMPED FROM a third floor unscathed man. That's some serious stunt you pulled Little Bird! Or should I say Big Bird!" said Sandy with real awe in his eyes. They got busy loading and organizing the food, water, and equipment onto the boat, and after everything was checked and accounted for they took a short nap before starting the big crossing at three in the morning.

All was quiet for the first few hours. The sun came up and it was a beautiful morning with good wind and little swell. A pod of dolphins joined them as they navigated onto the warm stream current. As they began to cross, they relished in the feeling of freedom and speed. Then, they saw lightning forming in the distance parallel to their course. Even though it was a beautiful sight in the daylight, Sandy's face dropped. "There must be a thunderstorm gathering somewhere close to us, bro. There can't be lightning without clouds."

As if summoned by Sandy's words, thunderclouds began to build ominously around them. Tiago started to regret jumping off the balcony the night before, and wished he was safely locked up in his grandparents' apartment. Cold gusts of wind from the north began picking up speed, and the sea around them darkened with swirling swaths of confused waves. Then came the rain. It spattered in huge drops on the water and on *Hope*, quickly growing into a downpour of piercing water bullets. The weather had completely changed in a matter of minutes.

Sandy sprung into action, making them put on their drysuits and life jackets, checking the charts and changing the course of the boat to try and skirt around the storm. Tiago helped where he could, but he was scared. The last time he had seen waves that big he had lost his entire family.

"It's okay, dude," said Sandy, patting Tiago on the back. "You know the saying… *Great voyages usually have bad beginnings.*" He paused, lost in thought, and then in a very business-like tone with almost no hint of his endearing drawl he explained. "Okay, the wind is against the current, so we just need to get off the stream."

Fog began to envelop them as they tried to redirect course, combined with the spray, it made it impossible to see past a metre. This was actually comforting for Tiago, as he could no longer watch the ten-metre waves threatening to break the bow.

They spent the rest of the day navigating like this; altering their course with the storm following right behind them. At night, things got worse. The wind picked up to forty-five knots and the waves grew even bigger. Tiago had gone down to the cabin to look for something, and heard Sandy calling him out to help on deck. As he climbed out to the helm, the boat jerked sideways and Tiago went flying head first over the side deck between the railings and into the ocean.

All went black. Tiago couldn't tell up from down and he was spinning. He couldn't breathe, couldn't see, couldn't move; it was as if he were dead already. Except he wasn't dead, he could still *feel*. He could feel his lungs compressing, feel the freezing water around him, and he could certainly feel his panic rising. He could also sense his life jacket struggling to push him up to the surface where his feet were; he was upside down. Tiago finally righted himself and kicked hard, reaching the surface just in time. He gulped all the air he could, and quite a bit of spray. He opened his eyes and saw the boat moving away from him, fast. Sandy was shouting something as he threw a lifeline, but it didn't make it to Tiago.

Sandy turned the boat around in a wide circle with marvellous skill and brought it back close to Tiago. Tiago had been lucky, as he had fallen into an eddy which kept him spinning more or less in the same place. Sandy threw the lifeline again from the stern, and this time Tiago was able to catch it. He would never forget the feeling of holding onto something in the middle of the darkness. He was inundated by that same tingling sensation of being alive and invincible. When he was a few metres from the boat he pulled hard on the rope and used the momentum to leap onto the vessel like a giant frog. Sandy couldn't believe what he saw, but was so overwhelmed with the emotion of getting his friend back, that he put the strange leap out of his mind. He brought Tiago into the cabin and resolved to get them out of the storm in one piece.

Sandy decided to get on the stream current again in the hope they could sail right through the storm and out the other side. Soon they were back on the current, still amid a violent thunderstorm, but sailing fast through the teeming rain. The fog lifted slowly and they began to see light as dawn approached. The wind calmed and the waves returned to a manageable size, and Tiago finally came back up on deck. As he looked to the sky a gentle gust of wind from the southwest wrapped itself around him, as if it were comforting him and telling him it was all over now.

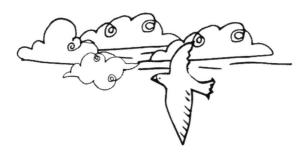

THIRTEEN

Abuela Moto

A BUELA MOTO STAYED ON the beach until the boat was lost in the horizon. When she couldn't see it any longer she focused and began to *feel* it, like a slight caress on the skin. There was Alba; *Abuela Moto* sensed her through the wind that she controlled. She hadn't done this since eight years ago when she heard the news of the shipwreck. A neighbour told her, and that her granddaughter had turned up on the west coast of the country. Before going to pick up Alba in Aguide, *Doña Coromoto* went to the beach and desperately searched with her mind for the rest of her family. She didn't feel either Cecilia nor Tiago and so assumed they had both perished.

But now, knowing from Alba that Tiago was alive, she realized that her gift was limited. It seemed to only work at sea and not on land. So she decided to search one more time. Perhaps, by luck, Tiago was in the water. She had an intuition; so she focused again and expanded her consciousness to the northwest. She went on and on until there, in the Atlantic Gulf Stream, she found her grandson. What *Abuela Moto* felt knowing that both Alba and Tiago were loose in the sea was bigger than her, than everything. She poured out her love for them and for her daughter who was gone. She emptied it into the breeze and blessed it, managing to stop the storm that was stalking Tiago and to help him cross the Atlantic without further problems. From now on, neither one of her two grandchildren would face bad weather on their journeys.

FOURTEEN

Alba

MOMENTS AFTER SHE LOST SIGHT of *Abuela Moto*, Alba cut the engine; she needed a second to steady herself. She looked up at the sky, the sun, the sea, and she started to feel all alone, but in a magical instant she noticed a slight easterly breeze enveloping her. Her hair ruffled, her clothes fluttered, and she laughed, knowing immediately it had been her grandmother. She started the engine and without needing to see the compass, she continued in the direction of the wind: northwest.

Alba cruised for almost five hours at a constant speed, and knew that she would soon reach La Tortuga. She spotted a small island on the horizon and decided to spend the night there. She anchored in a tiny bay away from the holiday yachts that packed the bigger bay and decided to jump in the water. Without a thought, she dove in and swam happily among the fish and live coral still left in that area, feeling that she completely belonged to the sea and thinking how silly she had been for not wanting to enter the water all these days. That night she slept peacefully on the beach and she woke up the next day ready to continue the search for her brother.

Her next destination was Cayo de Agua in Los Roques which, as its name indicated, had an underground source of fresh water where Alba could restock. This would be a longer trip and it would take the whole day to get there. Although it was early, the sun was hot so Alba put on her baseball hat, sticking all her hair inside, and she happily set off.

At noon, Alba decided to anchor to take a break. She was about twenty kilometers from La Orchila. This island was a Venezuelan military base filled with Chavista soldiers and was used as a vacation retreat by the Venezuelan president. Alba had heard many stories about the island, none of them good, and she wanted to avoid going near it at all costs. But it was too late. When she cut out her engine, she heard the sound of more and spotted a pair of boats rapidly approaching her. Thinking fast, she took the photo of her family out of the backpack and tucked it under her clothes inside her bathing suit. She saw the waterproof compass and decided to hang it around her neck under her t-shirt. She had just done this when the two boats began encircling her closely.

There were two men in one of the boats and a boy in the other. Alba knew without a doubt he was there to pilot away her *peñero* after it was stolen from her.

"Don't even think about moving, little boy!" Said the shorter of the two men.

They were Venezuelan pirates. Alba hesitated, but obeyed when she saw the gun tucked into the belt of the man who had spoken. She waited quietly while the two boats got closer and the taller man jumped onto her boat and tied it to his. She was terrified and had no idea what to do next - she had never been more scared in her life.

At that moment, her brother didn't exist, neither her grandma nor Marenos; she was only thinking about how to survive the next few minutes.

"And what are you doing so far from the shore kid?" Asked the pirate. "You are not fishing. Are you going for a ride?" He insisted as he walked around checking the boat. "What's in the backpack? Woah! A hundred dollars! Look, Edgar, we get a tip in addition to the *peñerito*!"

The man kept talking and asking Alba questions but she didn't listen to anything he said, she only saw how Edgar took a rope and passed it to the chatterbox; and then how he took her hands. A thought flashed through Alba's mind, *'Create the most space.'* A thought that brought back the memory of so many afternoons in *Las Luces*, practicing knots with her brother, tying and timing each other to see who undid their ropes faster. *'I have to grip my knuckles, one against the other, as much as I can, push with my palms and spread my elbows'* ... That was the trick to create the most space between her hands, making the rope looser and easier to undo later on.

To distract them, Alba asked Edgar, pointing at the boy, "Is he your son?"

Surprised, Edgar turned to the boy and looked at him with pride. "Yes, he is my son and this *peñero* is for him."

Rage ignited within Alba as she thought of *Abuela Moto*'s efforts to get this little boat for her. She took advantage of the fact that the man who tied her was also looking at Edgar and his son, and spread her elbows as much as she could.

"And what's your name?" Alba asked the boy.

"Pedro Luis," he answered with shame and sadness, and Alba realized that perhaps Pedro Luis was not there of his own free will. This fact did not temper her anger, but it focused her on what she had to do.

"Pedro Luis," she turned to him, "Take good care of my boat while you have it, because I *will* get it back." The two men looked at each other and were ready to explode with laughter when, very quickly, Alba pushed the tall man with all her strength to the bottom of the boat and taking the largest possible mouthful of air, dived into the sea.

FIFTEEN

—

Tiago

BY NIGHTFALL TIAGO AND SANDY were anchored in a quiet bay
south of Bone Fish Pond in Nassau. Since the crossing they
had sailed with a strong favourable wind and had been joined
by more dolphins. It was as if the deadly storm had never happened.

They spent that night and the next day anchored, resting, and
making repairs to the boat. Their plan was to keep cruising through
the Exumas, a Bahamian district of more than three-hundred
islands, and then sail between Cuba and Haiti towards Jamaica.

The next morning as Tiago was waking up, he had an odd feeling. Something wasn't right. The boat wasn't bobbing up and down
and swaying as it normally would and it was tilted on one side. This
could only mean one thing. He shook Sandy awake and he too instantly knew there was a problem.

"We are stuck Sandy," said Tiago looking out the porthole. They
were aground on a large sandbank.

"Rats, either the tide went down or we drifted," answered Sandy.
Check the GPS and compare our coordinates against last night's
log entry. I'll go outside and take a look."

Tiago checked, and found they had somehow drifted almost
sixty kilometres southeast to a large sandbank off the north coast

of Ship Channel Cay. He went on deck and saw Sandy was already busy checking for damage and leaks.

"We didn't set our anchor properly on the sand, or maybe the current reversed and the anchor didn't reset," lamented Sandy.

Perking up, he said, "Okay, this is what we need to do," his business-like voice back. "First, go down and take a look at the charts to see where the deep water is and what type of bottom we have here. I'm sure this is all sand, but we should be sure there is no coral or rock that could puncture the hull. Then, look over the tides. With any luck, we are in low tide now."

"Should we turn on the engine and see if we can reverse out of the sandbank?" Asked Tiago.

"That's the last thing we should do. We'll just stir up the bottom and make that sand go into our engine intake and clog it up," explained Sandy. If he hadn't noticed it during the storm, Tiago certainly saw it now. He realized that Sandy, at his young age, was already a sea dog and he really knew what he was talking about. Tiago decided to be the best hand he could be, and leave the important calls to his skipper.

They checked the charts, confirming that the bottom was sandy and that the deeper water was straight ahead. Unfortunately, the tide was high, so they needed to get out of this today; otherwise the low tide going out the next day would sandbank them even more. They agreed on a simple plan: to *kedge off* the boat. This meant pulling the vessel into the deeper water using a spare, or kedge anchor. They would attach the small anchor to the boat's winch, and place it on the dinghy. Then they would take it to deeper water, drop it, and pull the boat. Every metre or so, they would retrieve the anchor from the bottom and drop it further out,

repeating the whole operation over and over, until the sailboat was free.

They pointed the vessel to the deeper water and began working. Placing the heavy anchor on the dinghy was no easy task, but they managed it. Tiago remained on *Hope* and Sandy went out on the dinghy. Tiago waited for his signal and cranked the winch. The boat inched forward. They did it again, and again, very carefully and very slowly. It took all day to move less than ten metres.

They stopped before sunset to take a rest, both exhausted. Devoting an entire day to lowering and lifting an anchor in and out of the water and cranking a winch – after surviving a storm – was not what they had in mind for their first Caribbean sailing adventure. Feeling a little defeated, they sat on the bow of the sailboat to eat two sad-looking sandwiches Tiago had made.

Gazing at the shore, they noticed a blur of pink and black. They were sure they were seeing flamingos and relaxed to watch. But it wasn't birds. There were a dozen little bodies huddled up running towards the boat. Pigs! The cutest, fattest, happiest little pigs either of them had ever seen. Tiago and Sandy were amazed. They had heard about the Exumas swimming pigs, but never thought they would show up in this very cay, and right when they really needed a smile.

The next hour was spent playing, feeding, and best of all, swimming with the amazing creatures. They even stayed around in the water when Tiago and Sandy finally decided to get back to work. Either it was their newfound strength after a good break, or the magic of the swimming pigs, but in only two tries the boat was freed and they celebrated with one last dip with their new friends.

In the water surrounded by piggies, Tiago felt there could be no wrong in the world, that their misfortunes were in the past, and that the Caribbean Sea was truly his home.

SIXTEEN

Alba

THE SEA WAS ONLY FOUR METERS DEEP and there was no coral, algae, or big rocks to hide in. Alba stuck herself upside down to her *peñero's* hull like a starfish. Doing this with her hands tied up was a very difficult task as she could only use the strength of her legs. She saw streaks crossing the water diagonally around her; bullets. She waited, and when she was almost out of breath, she watched with relief as the boats finally dislodged from her *peñero* and their propellers began spinning. The two boats went away in the same direction they had come. Then, the engine of her own boat started and Alba quickly broke off, kicking the hull hard to push herself towards the bottom and avoid the blades.

Edgar and his friend didn't understand where the *boy* had gone, but they were in a hurry and had already got what they wanted. Anyway, even if he was alive, they knew he wouldn't last long so they decided to leave and go on with their business. Pedro Luis was left to bring the *peñero* back. When he started the engine he heard a strong blow in the bottom of the boat and, looking out over the water, he saw the boy descending like a torpedo towards the bottom of the sea. At that moment, Pedro Luis felt a mixture of admiration and envy and decided once and for all to stop helping his father. He would escape one day, he had to plan it properly, but for now he would help the kid. It was the least he could do. He found a water bottle on the boat and threw it into the sea next to the hat that had fallen off the kid's head when he jumped in. In half an hour, when he could get away from his dad, he would come back for the kid and return his boat to him. He left quickly so the kid could come up for air - he must have been under for a few minutes already!

Alba could only hold out a moment longer at the bottom, her lungs feeling like they were folding over inside of her. She swam up as fast as she could, and as she surfaced she gulped the air in giant bites. She watched the boats cruise away and felt panic instead of relief. She did not want to be left alone. In that moment she would rather have them return and take her instead of abandoning her in the middle of the sea. She screamed as loudly as she could, kicked, and cried. She frantically tried to break free, but the only thing she managed to do was swallow a whole lot of water. This went on for a few minutes until she realized that anger, at this moment, was not helping her at all. It had given her the courage to jump off the boat, but now what she needed to do was to calm down, think clearly, and act very deliberately.

Although she couldn't swim well with her hands tied, she tried to relax by thinking of how lucky she was to be alive and by letting herself feel the excitement about one day, maybe soon, seeing her brother. The thought briefly crossed her mind that if she was really Marena, there was no better time than now for her ability to kick in. But she dropped the notion as soon as she began despairing again because nothing was happening. When she managed to refocus and slow down her breathing, she decided to dive once more so she could untie the knots while sitting on the sand. She went down to the bottom, picked up a medium stone, sat cross-legged, and placed the stone on her legs. She began to work on the ropes using her teeth and the stone. Every time she ran out of air, she would go up, float on the surface, relax, and dive down again. After several trips up and down, she managed to undo the knots. This achievement made her feel so much better. She was still alone in the middle of the Caribbean, but she had managed to free her hands and now she had full use of her strong body.

She took off her t-shirt and shorts, wearing only her blue bathing suit. She still had her family photo safely tucked under it. She went down one last time to hide her clothes under the stone, just in case. When she came up she finally saw her cap floating a few meters away along with her water bottle – it must have fallen off the boat in the commotion. Finding the bottle encouraged her even more. She drank some water, and carefully tucked the bottle and hat around her waist, securing them with the rope. Now she was ready to go. But as soon as she started swimming, she realized she had a new problem: the closest shore was crawling with Chavista soldiers.

SEVENTEEN

Tiago

A FEW DAYS HAD PASSED SINCE Tiago and Sandy's epic swim with the little pigs. They were now bordering the southeastern side of Cuba. There were two reasons Tiago and Sandy needed to avoid checking in with the port authorities. The first being that Tiago was a minor, and the second that Sandy – who was also a minor but had a fake ID, was American and the cross-border relations between the two countries were lukewarm at best.

They spotted a beautiful deserted bay to anchor for the night, dotted with coral reefs and crystal blue waters. They whiled away the warm afternoon swimming and spearfishing in the shallow reefs. Then they grilled their catch, ate their fill, and went to bed. In the middle of the night Sandy woke Tiago and told him he was going for a dip to cool off. Tiago also felt hot, but was more interested in snoozing than swimming. He fell back into a deep sleep until he was awakened again by Sandy's shouts.

Tiago ran up on deck and stared at the water trying to find Sandy. He followed the sound of his voice towards the shore and saw the light of Sandy's headlamp shining in the water about a hundred metres away.

"What's wrong, Sandy?" he shouted, grabbing a flashlight.

"Sharks! Tiger sharks, I think."

Tiago's blood froze. Tiger sharks were common in the Caribbean and had a reputation for eating just about anything, including license plates and land dwelling animals like cats; yes, cats! They were also nighttime feeders with possibly the best eyesight of all sharks. They were aggressive, and capable of eating large prey. And while Tiago knew shark attacks were extremely uncommon, he also knew Sandy was in serious danger.

"Where are they? Can you see them?" Tiago called out.

"Yes. They are between me and the boat. I'm standing on a reef," answered Sandy.

"Go to shore," shouted Tiago. "Spend the night there, and they'll be gone by morning."

"I can't," answered Sandy, "They are stalking a turtle, man. She's beautiful. I need to help her!"

Tiago felt his entire body shaking from top to bottom. He was filled with an intense desire to jump straight for Sandy, land on the reef, grab him, and lift him back to the safety of the boat. He saw it like a movie in his mind. He climbed over the railing, extended his arms and… he stopped himself suddenly, almost falling overboard. 'What's wrong with me?,' he thought.

"Throw me the snorkeling bag! Quick! They are circling around her, and they'll be going in soon!" yelled Sandy.

"Let them be! This is nature, it's the way it works," answered Tiago desperately.

"I need to help her. I don't know why, but I just do! I'm going in with or without the gear, now throw the stuff or I will start swimming without it," shouted Sandy in that same bossy voice that only came on when he was in absolute control of a situation.

Tiago obeyed. He ran to the bow, picked up a small bag with a mask and flippers, and with all his strength and focus, threw it straight to Sandy. It landed with a splash quite close to him, and he quickly swam to grab it before it sank.

Tiago ran back and turned on the stern light, shining it in Sandy's direction. It flooded the area and he saw it, a giant turtle well over two metres long, being circled by two sharks, each twice the turtle's length.

EIGHTEEN

Alba

LBA HAD NO CHOICE but to swim towards the island. She knew she could not stay floating around for much longer and that her only hope for survival was to swim towards shore. She swam for hours and hours. Anyone else, with a normal body, would have succumbed to the sun and dehydration, not to mention the exhaustion from such great effort. But Alba was special, her body was different, and most of all, her mind. She focused on one stroke at a time, moved little by little, drank water only every hour, and if she got tired she would go down to the bottom to sit and feel the sand underneath her.

After four hours, her eyes began to burn and she had to close them and swim blindly, checking her course from time to time. She would open them a little, fighting the pain, to look at the compass on her neck. She continued swimming this way all afternoon and in her delirium did not even notice the sun setting.

It was late at night and she had been swimming for more than eight hours when she heard a familiar noise: small waves lapping the shore. She clung to that sound and splashed toward it with the last of her strength. She felt something hard pressing against her belly and with all the joy in the world she flattened herself against the rocks jutting out of the sea. She crawled the last few meters out of the water onto a huge stone, and there she lay until the next morning.

The first thing she did when she opened her eyes was throw up. She hadn't eaten anything in almost a day, so it was mostly water flying out of her body. The sun was high in the sky and Alba was without any shade or protection. She felt like an egg frying on a pan. The vegetation was arid without trees that could save her from the sun. She spotted a small cave made by three large stones leaning on each other and crawled into its shadow, still unable to stand up. In the shade she felt better, she took out the rest of the water and finished it without thinking much about what came next. She sat recovering for a couple more hours until she decided to explore and check to see if the soldiers were around, and try to find something to eat.

Standing up was a difficult task made up of several attempts and as many falls because her legs were cramping up. Alba thought about how lucky she had been not to have suffered one of these cramps at sea. She was ecstatic to have survived the pirates and the water, and felt an enormous pride. She thought of her grandmother, who would have been proud too. Finally, she managed to get up and start walking. She read the compass and fixed the position in her mind. Although it was an inhospitable place, this spot was sheltered and so she wanted to return there for the night. She began climbing the steep slope to get a better view.

Alba moved slowly to not exert herself too much, up and up the hill until she reached an edge and carefully peered out, and what she saw was terrifying. At her feet, barely a kilometer away, was a military base with dozens of sheds, and beyond, a marina full of green boats. Hundreds of armed soldiers were at the base doing military drills. There were also about twenty tanks, and a huge ship docked at a distance. At that moment, Alba heard a roar followed by a helicopter landing on the base. Although she was scared, she couldn't help but smile because the scene was totally chaotic. Overwhelmed by the heat, the soldiers did the exercises poorly, it was obvious that many of the tanks were not working and the helicopter did not know where to land, almost running over several soldiers in its indecision. This military base was a mess. Still, there were hundreds of soldiers and they would easily find her if she stayed on the island much longer.

NINETEEN

Tiago

OTH THE TURTLE AND THE SHARKS were close to the surface of the water, with the turtle sticking her head out to breathe every now and then. One of the sharks quickly burst towards her, but with great agility the turtle maneuvered around it and bit its gills. The other shark came at her, and the turtle flipped onto her side, perpendicular to the shark, using the bony plates of her carapace as a shield. By being on her side, the shark wasn't able to fit her shell inside its mouth. Tiago searched for Sandy who was so engrossed by the action that he had moved in dangerously close to the fight. Then, both sharks charged at the turtle at the same time and Sandy sped through the water in their direction.

The sharks and turtle moved in a convoluted circular-like dance, with the turtle purposely staying so close to them they could not angle themselves to reach her with their teeth. She was winning for the moment, but it wasn't going to last. Sandy, with surprising speed, came from the side of one of the sharks and stuck his hand into its gills. It was enough of an annoyance to get the shark off the turtle's trail. The shark swam away fast and reappeared on the other side of the turtle. Sandy then jabbed at the other shark with his hand. This little game went on for a while; as soon as one shark retreated, Sandy would face off against the other one, but seconds later the first shark would return to the fight. Slowly, the turtle began to comprehend that Sandy wasn't a threat, and was actually fighting for her. They positioned themselves close to each other, and continued to move in a circle, biting, jabbing, and even punching at the sharks.

Again, they were winning, but not for long. Tiago could see Sandy was getting tired. He was moving slower and was coming up for air more often. The sharks were closing in. It was only a matter of minutes now and it would all be over for Sandy and the turtle. Tiago made up his mind; he grabbed the flare gun from the emergency kit, loaded it, and aimed at the fight as far from Sandy as he could. He fired. The next thing his hand was in agony; the flare had dripped molten slag onto it but he would have to worry about his painful burn later. The flare had no effect and he felt very foolish watching it fizzle out in the water... fire needs oxygen to burn. He knew that, but he had acted too quickly and now he was injured.

He was desperate, and certain that Sandy was going to be killed helping the turtle. It would be an honourable and fitting death, but quite stupid in Tiago's view. He thought fast – the sharks were just too powerful and dangerous to fight in close combat, even for Sandy and Tiago together. They needed some kind of advantage. Then it came to him, and the answer was unexpectedly simple: the boat!

He checked the depth of the surrounding area on the boat's computer. It was shallow where the fight was taking place, but there was just enough clearance for the keel. He started the engine and throttled forward to retrieve the anchor. He had the difficult task of doing everything by himself, but he tried to keep calm and focus on each step. He ran back to the stern and began reversing the boat towards where the fight was taking place. There was no way he could warn Sandy, and anyway, he didn't want to distract him. He manoeuvred with extra care, switching between reverse-throttle and neutral, until he could no longer get closer without the risk of hitting Sandy with the rudder. He left the boat in neutral, ran right up next to Sandy's head and unceremoniously grabbed him, pulling him up onto the platform. Sandy had no idea what had happened. Before he could say anything, Tiago ran back to the throttle and spun the boat around in one swift circle with the intention of dispersing the fight below and allowing the turtle a chance to escape

At this point Sandy began yelling. "What are you doing, dude? You are going to run us into the reef!"

"It's okay, trust me, we are deep enough," answered Tiago, waiting for the bossy retort that never came. Sandy was distracted; as he was searching with the stern light he saw a pair of fins heading out of the shallows. Then, pointing the light towards the shore, he spotted a beautiful giant turtle pushing herself slowly out of the sea and onto the sand; her back left leg limp.

"And she lived, she lived… how very swell," he whispered before passing out with a big grin.

TWENTY

Alba

ALBA WAS WATCHING the military base carefully, trying to find out where the kitchen was located in the giant complex. A bell rang and all the soldiers ran to the building closest to Alba. When half a dozen dogs showed up and followed the soldiers, Alba knew it was lunchtime and the food she wanted so much was in that building. She returned to her cave to get some sleep and wait until nightfall.

She woke in the middle of the night; a crescent moon was high in the sky and the stars were shining everywhere. It was a clear night, beautiful, but far from ideal for her mission. Alba dove into the sea, both to wake herself up and to shake off her nerves. She came out of the water feeling determined, scaling the large black rocks and up the slope on all fours. Wearing only her blue bathing suit, she looked like a sea creature emerging from the water for the first time.

She reached the top of the hill and looked around her. All was quiet and she began her descent with stealth, making almost no noise with her bare feet. She felt a presence behind her and turned around quickly; there were two of the dogs she had seen earlier. They

didn't look dangerous; on the contrary, they seemed sad. Relieved, Alba called out to them. They came happily and allowed themselves to be petted, delighted by the attention. Alba imagined they too were very hungry and thought they could help on her mission and share in the loot, if there was one.

The two dogs followed Alba silently toward the shed. Alba tried to open the door, but it was locked. To the right of the door, a little above its lintel, she saw a small window that was ajar. She stepped back, gathered momentum, and jumped off to the low edge. With her strong arms she lifted the rest of her body and pushed open the window, sliding gently inside. The dogs were still looking up in admiration when Alba opened the door for them. They entered a dark hallway and Alba led the dogs into the room with the window, which turned out to be the kitchen. The dogs went straight to a large metal box: the refrigerator. Alba opened it and the trio proceeded to devour everything they could.

They were almost ready to go when Alba caught a glimpse of another door in the back of the kitchen. She opened without effort and discovered a room crammed with large boxes of medicines, diapers, alcohol, and cigarettes: contraband. She understood right away that the Venezuelan army was at the centre of all of the corruption and crime in her country. She felt anger again, and helplessness.

She closed the door and started going back through the kitchen when she thought of a little mischief that might make her feel better. In one corner of the kitchen there was a coffee station ready for the morning: twelve huge pots with ground coffee ready to be brewed, and the same number of containers filled with sugar. Alba proceeded to empty the sugar containers – the dogs ate all the sugar – and filled them all with salt. She remembered seeing some bags of planting soil near the entrance. Throwing the coffee in the garbage under all the trash, she filled the filters with the dirt. Now they were ready to go. Alba took some cans of tuna and several bottles of water and the three new friends returned happily to her little camp.

Early in the morning, Alba looked out to see the Chavista soldiers sleepwalking into the shed eager to enjoy their morning coffee. She waited a few minutes until she happily heard their outcries of disgust.

TWENTY ONE

Tiago

"T HAT WAS EPIC, BRO," sighed Sandy, checking Tiago's mangled hand. They were making their way now to Port Antonio, Jamaica, where they would take Tiago to a doctor, get more supplies and refuel the boat.

"Wasn't that just amazing? I mean I really thought that was it: that I, Alexander Shores, would die honourably right there helping a noble sea creature, and then, boom! You pulled me out of the water and scared off the sharks all at once! I've never felt so alive, man." He stood up and shouted. "I am the king of the sea!"

Tiago was silent. He was still a bit mad at Sandy, and in a considerable amount of pain, but secretly he felt like a king himself for having saved his friend. "I guess we are even now. We've both pulled each other out of the water," he finally said.

A few hours later Sandy checked in with customs, having dropped off Tiago first at a close-by cove in order to avoid registering him as a minor. After clearing customs, Sandy picked up Tiago and they moored at the new marina. It was a little expensive for them, but they were craving real food and firm land so they decided to stay overnight and enjoy themselves.

Port Antonio was just what they needed, a bustling little town that seemed like a huge metropolis after days of sailing. Tiago saw a doctor who treated his burns and prescribed him painkillers. He told him he'd have full use of his hand in no time. Maybe because he was hurt, or perhaps because he was back in civilization, Tiago missed his adoptive parents intensely and pulled out his phone to call them.

He was interrupted by Sandy. "I know where we are going to have dinner, just need to make a call," said Sandy, grabbing Tiago's phone. "Wah gwaan Dickie! It's Sandy-man. Yeah, tonight, me and my friend." Sandy burst into laughter. "For two, I mean. Thenk yuh Dickie, likkle muore!" Sandy hung up. "Oh Dickie, he's so funny. Okay, let's go rent bikes."

They made their way out of town along a beautiful coastal road surrounded by lush vegetation. After only seeing blue for so long, Tiago's senses were very aware of the emerald leaves on the trees surrounding them. They arrived at Dickie's place, a ramshackle building on the shore, and greeted its owner, an old white-bearded fellow with kind eyes, only half of his teeth, and a black toque perfectly perched on his dreadlocks. "So, this is the little bird," he said to Sandy looking at Tiago and they both laughed again. Tiago didn't get the joke but liked Dickie right away.

They had a fun night; eating their fill and laughing so hard food came out of their noses. They stayed for many hours. It was late and Tiago was getting sleepy. Sandy suddenly became very serious and said to Tiago, "Bro, we need to talk." Tiago's heart stopped. He had been waiting for 'the talk' from Sandy for a while – the one where Sandy, having had enough of storms, and sandbanks, and sharks, would tell Tiago they should part ways. Tiago braced himself for the upsetting words to come, but all of the bracing in the world could not prepare him for what he heard next. "Tiago, I think you can fly."

TWENTY TWO

Alba

THE FOLLOWING WEEK WAS ONE of the most peaceful and fun for Alba since she found out her brother was alive. Pepe and Pepito, as she had called the two dogs, became her loyal followers, and Alba was grateful for their company on this lonely journey. Every night they stole food, explored the camp a little more, and carried out a little mischief. Alba delighted in the idea that, although she could not - yet - change things in Venezuela, she could take small actions to inconvenience the daily lives of those who oppressed her country.

Alba and her friends had also extensively explored their side of the island and made an incredible find: a sea cave. They discovered it literally by accident. They were walking on the rocks while Alba told the dogs some entertaining story without looking where she was going. In an instant she took a step into the air and in another she descended rapidly into the void. Luckily, she fell into the middle of a beautiful cobalt pool. The cave was filled with the light streaming in from above, and Alba could truly appreciate its beauty. Far from being scared and thinking about how she was going to get out, she was filled with peace and joy, feeling like nothing bad could ever happen between these rock walls. Pepe and Pepito, seeing her so happy, decided to jump and share in the excitement. The three of them swam happily for a while until they decided to look for a way out. They found a tiny crack in which they could barely fit. It opened to the sea across the bay from the military marina.

Since discovering the cave, Alba returned to it daily, sometimes two or three times in the same day. Inside it she sensed something very special: the presence of her mother. She didn't know why; perhaps because she felt protected and sheltered in its waters, the way she used to feel in her mother's arms. She would let her thoughts wander and bit by bit her mind began opening up until she could finally re-examine the conversation she had had with her grandmother. She thought a lot about Marenos, her mother, and about herself. She asked herself questions and tried to answer them calmly, making her own deductions, abandoning anger and replacing it with curiosity. For the first time she wondered if her mother must have had a good reason for drowning, and so she decided to forgive her and to trust and feel protected by her again. Every time Alba left the cave, she was more certain that she was indeed Marena.

Meanwhile in the military camp, if there was chaos before, now there was complete disarray thanks to the actions of the three friends. The soldiers were very afraid. One of them, originally from *Los Llanos*, had convinced a large number of his colleagues that *La Sayona* herself was on the island to punish them one by one. Legend from *Los Llanos* has it that the specter of a woman dressed in white with long, straight, black hair appears at night to harass those who deserve it. With the exception of the night guards, no one went out at night, not even to go to the bathroom. They were certain that they would meet *La Sayona*.

The legend of *La Sayona* suited Alba wonderfully. Now she would walk with the dogs wearing a long white shirt she had found in the laundry room, and three black garbage bags strategically held over her head to look like long, shiny, straight hair. Up close, she looked very comical, but from a distance she was a true *Sayona*. As soon as her silhouette became visible on the hill at dusk the men would climb into their beds and stay there until morning.

General Ceballos was the only one who did not believe in *La Sayona*. He knew someone was wreaking havoc on account of the innocence of his soldiers. He had to get this over with right away, before it got out of hand. He called in three of his most faithful lieutenants and ordered them not to rest until they found the culprit.

That night Alba slept soundly, her heart happy and her belly full of an excellent dinner. Pepe and Pepito laid fast asleep by her side. Suddenly she heard a noise and before she could even open her eyes, she felt a hand quickly and tightly cover her mouth.

TWENTY THREE

Tiago

"CLOSE YOUR MOUTH AND HEAR me out, bro," said Sandy. "You told me when you were little they found you perched up on the boat's broken mast, right? Then, last week you jumped out of a third story, right? And a few days ago I saw you with my own eyes fly up from the water onto the boat!"

Tiago laughed hard for a long time until he was finally able to speak. "Sandy, you *are* crazy! I obviously climbed up that mast, and last week's jump was exactly that, a JUMP. And I leapt from the water, I didn't fly. I used all my strength to pull off the rope and jumped onboard. This conversation is delusional, man. Only you would come up with something like that!"

"Well, it isn't just me. Dickie, come here!" called out Sandy. The old man came to their table. "Whaddup?"

"Tell Tiago what you told me earlier, please?" asked Sandy.

"Well," Dickie began in his thick Jamaican accent, "There be these sacred sea protectors, some still alive, but most gone now. They breathe underwater and fly and command the winds. I met one. He lived underwater, truly, it was his home, I saw it. It had a bed and everything. He'd come here from time to time and eat with me and then back under he'd go. I say maybe you can fly, maybe you can't. I'd believe it because I've seen many things. I say you try at least. Worst thing you'll fall and hit your head. But if I'd be you, I'd be wanting to know, so I'd hit my head no problem to find out. And that's my story."

Sandy was looking at Tiago as if that was all the proof they needed, as if Dickie had presented them with irrefutable evidence. Having had enough, Tiago got up. "Thank you, Dickie, for your story and for dinner. I'm very tired. I'm going back to the boat. Sandy, the bill is yours. Good night."

Back in the boat, Tiago couldn't fall asleep. He felt ambushed by crazy people. His reality had completely shifted, from trying to find his sister with someone he trusted and considered somewhat sane, to being put in a very uncomfortable situation by that same person. Sandy was acting like a child, and so Tiago would have to treat him like one. He would gently explain to him that humans can't fly, even though it is the ultimate dream, a dream that he had almost every night; a dream where he was so close to his beloved stars, where he climbed ever higher and higher, and where he felt the wind within himself, as though it was pushing right through him and propelling him further... '*Spot it Tiago,*' he thought, scolding himself. He would have to explain to Sandy that humans can't fly – no matter how much they want to.

"Tiago," Sandy said as he came into the cabin, "I'm so sorry, bud, back in the restaurant... I was raving. Too much punch. Dickie and his stories got to me. I'm really sorry man."

"It's okay, Sandy," answered Tiago, shrugging his shoulders. Now he was too tired to talk.

"Really? You cool? Great, what a relief!" Answered Sandy sitting next to him.

"Yeah, let's just keep the crazy inside our own heads for a bit," said Tiago with a smile.

"You got it Little Bird! Hey, does that mean you'll pay for half the dins? It was pricey dude. Dickie even charged us for the napkins. He said they were imported from Copenhagen!" They both exploded with laughter and Sandy gave Tiago a great big hug; and just like that, all was back to normal between them.

But inside Tiago's mind, things were not back to normal. He looked out at the night sky and felt that tingling, electric current throughout his body. He began to wonder if maybe, perhaps, conceivably, there was a chance that what Sandy said could have some truth to it.

TWENTY FOUR

Alba

WHEN SHE OPENED HER EYES, Alba could only see a human silhouette against the light of the moon.

"Don't scream. Please," said a familiar voice, as the hand left her mouth. "Pedro Luis? Aren't you the pirate's son?" Alba exclaimed with surprise.

"Shhhhh, yes it's me, but please don't speak loudly, they're very close," replied Pedro Luis, allowing himself to be licked by the two dogs who had already decided that the young man did not pose any danger.

"Explain to me what you're doing here! Is your father on the island too? Where is my *peñero*? And... *who* is very close?" Alba demanded, sitting up and trying very hard not to show how scared she was.

"Calm down boy..." But then he looked at her closely, at her long curly hair and her blue bathing suit, and he paused a little confused. "Sorry, please calm down. Yes, my dad is on the island and so is your *peñero*. I went back to look for you that day, I knew you were under the boat and I left you the water. I didn't find you and since then I have been looking for you to give you back your little boat. I'm not like my dad, I promise you. I just don't know how to get away from him... You got away from him though, and so... I want to help you."

"How did you know I was here?" Alba asked, sitting down again.

"I always come to La Orchila with my father, he is a friend of *General Ceballos* and he brings him rum and cigarettes. I saw you one night dressed like *La Sayona*, and I knew it was you. And now the *General* has three of his men on your trail, and that's why I rushed to find you tonight. To warn you." Pedro Luis explained, adding, "By the way, how did you get here? Who picked you up from the water?"

"No one picked me up! I swam for hours and hours, went blind and almost drowned, thanks to your dad."

"Impossible! No one can swim that far, it must have been more than twenty kilometers. Perhaps an Olympic swimmer, or one of those triathlon guys, but not a girl..." Pedro Luis pondered aloud.

"What difference does it make if I'm a girl? Besides, I'm not a girl anymore, I'm going to be fifteen soon... Anyway, the fact is that I did swim without anyone's help and I've been stranded here since YOU took my boat!" Roared Alba.

"Forgive me, I'm really sorry," Pedro Luis recovered quickly. If it had been daylight, Alba would have seen the boy's flushed cheeks.

"Well, I believe you and I accept your help for now, but I still don't trust you," replied Alba. "Okay," Pedro Luis agreed. "You have to leave the island as soon as possible, because they will find you.

Right now, if you can. Your *peñero* is in the marina. I will go with you and take you wherever you want. You come from Margarita right? Your backpack has a Macanao sticker." He said, handing her the stolen backpack.

"Yes," Alba answered, checking the bag and seeing that her things were still there. She was so happy to find her sweater and put it on right away. "But I'm going alone, Pedro Luis. If Edgar finds out you are helping me, he's going to lynch you. Besides, someone has to take care of Pepe and Pepito." Alba looked at the dogs tenderly. "Help me get to the *peñero* and we'll leave it at that."

"Deal," answered the boy, knowing it was impossible to argue. "Can I ask you what your name is?"

"No, not yet." Alba replied.

They got up and packed the few things that Alba had accumulated in her short stay on the island: *La Sayona's* costume, two blankets for sleeping, some cans of tuna and a couple bottles of water. Suddenly, Pedro Luis raised his head, looked into the distance, and pointed up the hill, three circles of light were rapidly coming towards them.

In a matter of minutes, the soldiers would reach them. Alba pulled Pedro Luis in the direction of the cave and they ran. The soldiers saw them and rushed after them. Although Alba was barefoot, she stepped with agility on the rough rocks without feeling any pain. After going for so long without shoes, the soles of her feet were as hard as leather. They ran at full force towards the edge of the great hole and Alba jumped in, grabbing Pedro Luis by the shirt. At that moment, the poor boy was sure his story would end right there. The four of them fell into the luminous waters of the cave and scrambled to hide, pressing themselves against the darker walls. As soon as the water became still, three flashlights appeared above them.

The men peered into the cave and only saw the deep waters. They weren't sure if the kids had jumped in or not, but since none of the three wanted to launch themselves into the unknown they decided the kids must have kept running and they resumed their chase.

Alba and Pedro Luis waited for a while until all was quiet above, and then headed to the cave's exit. Their plan was to swim straight to *El Guácharo*, which was about four hundred meters from them. But as they peered through the crack that opened out to sea, they saw at least a dozen military boats between themselves and the marina, patrolling the entire bay and sporting huge flood lights. If they started swimming now towards the boat, they would be easily caught. They had no choice but to spend the night in the cave.

TWENTY FIVE

Tiago

TIAGO AND SANDY DECIDED to stay a couple more days in Port Antonio; Tiago would happily pay for the expenses as he still had plenty of funds from the sale of his Laser, plus he still owed Sandy for half of their expensive dinner. In the morning, Tiago took his rental bike and went for a ride along the coast heading west. He passed Dickie's restaurant and went through some small neighbourhoods. He veered off the pavement and went on a small gravel road that cut through beautiful green fields filled with big trees on the rolling hills. He saw a large open space the size of a soccer field and stopped.

Sitting on the edge of the field, he felt homesick. He missed his adoptive parents and wondered what they were going through at that moment: Were they mad? Did they miss him? Were they trying to find him? Did his grandparents feel guilty? He remembered that night, jumping out of their balcony and feeling so much joy. It really was a big jump – three stories was about nine metres – and he didn't fall straight down but in a big arch. He took his phone out of his backpack. And he saw, feeling the guilt build up again in his stomach, that he had one hundred and seven missed calls.

He searched online: *What happens if you jump from three stories?* The answer: *If you survive you'll more than likely break both of your legs, blow out your knees, compress your spine, break your ribs, and get a nasty concussion.*

Tiago flinched. If he had googled it that night he would never have jumped. But he did jump, and not only did he survive unscathed but it had been a fun, even thrilling, experience and something he could do again if necessary. Could it be then, that perhaps he was built differently than other people? That he could jump really far; not *fly*, but jump? He got up and looked at the phone again, seeing once more the number of unanswered calls. Feeling more remorse than he could handle, he dropped the phone and ran straight across the field. Halfway across, he jumped, reaching for the other side, and just like that, he flew.

TWENTY SIX

Alba

SPENDING AN ENTIRE NIGHT IN A DARK and damp cave was a nightmare for Pedro Luis. He was wet and freezing and could not get comfortable, laying on a small rock between Pepe and Pepito. The two dogs were already used to the adventurous life with Alba. They had gained quite a bit of weight and their coats were shiny. They walked upright, and they no longer had sad faces but rather wore a proud and even mischievous look. They knew something dangerous was happening, but they also fully trusted that Alba would protect them. They slept close to Pedro Luis to keep warm, lifting their heads from time to time to check on Alba who was dozing in the water.

For her, spending an entire night wet in a cave was no problem. She fell asleep almost instantly, floating in the water, quickly returning to the sleep that Pedro Luis had interrupted. She was awakened by the light of dawn and she went to see if the boats had left. They were still there, between her and her *peñero*. Suddenly she felt a presence in the water below her. She tried to see the bottom and spotted a large shadow moving slowly far below. At first she thought it was a shark, but Alba, being Alba, was not scared; she stayed still and kept watching. After a while, when the sun fully appeared through the great opening above, the water turned iridescent blue and Alba clearly saw a beautiful giant sea turtle swimming below her.

Alba took a breath and dove to get closer to her. And there it was, as if waiting for her. Alba noticed that one of its hind legs was smaller than the others and a little bent; and yet it was still the most beautiful creature she had ever seen. The turtle slowly approached her and touched Alba's nose with its nose. Immediately, Alba knew that Tiago was in the Caribbean and that he was heading towards her. She knew it with the same certainty that she was Marena. The turtle had communicated with her, she had *told* her.

The large animal swam in circles several times around Alba and then glided towards one of the crevices. Alba understood: it was time to leave the cave. She rose to the surface, realizing she had been under a long time, and then woke up the others. They ate the two cans of tuna they had left and began to swim towards the marina. Before exiting through the crack, Alba looked once more into the depth of the cave and said, "I promise I will find him."

TWENTY SEVEN

Tiago

.

TIAGO LAY ON THE GRASS catching his breath and looking up at the morning sky. He could feel his hand throbbing a little. Had he really done it? Had he been up in the air for a few seconds? Or had he imagined it? Had he wished it to happen so bad that he made it all up? What was going on with him? Why couldn't he explain this? He heard footsteps and looked over to see Sandy approaching. It was funny; watching his friend on the green turf was almost disconcerting. Sandy belonged to the sea and only the sea. Was it the same with Tiago? Did he belong to the air and only the air?

"Hey bud, I thought I'd come make sure you weren't getting into any trouble," said Sandy laying down next to Tiago. "What are we thinking about, bro?"

"I am thinking… I am thinking that maybe I *can* fly," stammered Tiago. "Or at least jump really far. I just did it. I was in the air for a couple of seconds and covered about four metres until I landed on my bad hand. Or at least I think I did… I don't know, maybe I'm losing my mind."

"No, you are not! This is amazing!" Sandy got up and said in his business voice. "Show me what you got."

Tiago was so very tired. He didn't think he had any more air-time left in him, but he wanted to show his friend. He needed it to be real, and the only way for it to be was to have a witness, someone to tell him he wasn't daydreaming. He ran as hard as he could and jumped – then fell flat on the ground. He tried again and again, always with the same result. He kept on trying without saying a word to Sandy, but each time it ended the same way: with him on the ground. Finally, Sandy walked over and hugged Tiago. He wanted to comfort him, but also keep him from trying again. "You are so tired, bro. I think we should go home to the boat and rest."

Tiago began sobbing like he never had before. He didn't understand why. He was just so weary and felt so many things at the same time: hope and despair, love and guilt, freedom and confinement, wonder and disbelief. But worst of all, he felt uncertainty, and for him this was the single most dreadful feeling he could bear. He had felt it all those weeks at the hospital in Willemstad when he was seven years old and he was all alone after losing his family, not understanding where he was, the language they spoke, or what would become of him. He had promised himself he would never feel that way again, no matter what he had to do to protect himself. Now, he didn't even know who he was or if he was right in his mind, and it was overwhelmingly scary. He took a deep breath. He needed to get on top of that feeling. "One more try, Sandy."

"Dunno bud. Your legs... you can't even run anymore," answered his friend.

"Yeah, you are right. I'll climb."

He found a big tree, about seven metres tall, and began climbing. Sandy was surprised by his agility, even as tired as Tiago was, he looked elegant and deliberate, like a lizard moving up the tree. Tiago reached the top, but instead of looking down, he gazed north to the green and blue expanse around him. He thought about his sister. Where was she? Could she be close? Maybe she was even on her way to him? He found it curious that he had just thought that, but maybe she also knew he was alive. Maybe she was the one who was going to rescue *him*. Curiously, he thought about Sandy's turtle too, wondering where she was, and thinking it was funny that both Sandy and him believed the turtle was a *she*. She had won against all odds; she had survived. He chuckled to himself thinking about how a turtle and a human could survive two sharks... Slowly, the feelings of love, hope, freedom, and wonder began pushing the others aside – just a little bit. Tiago closed his eyes and let himself go.

He kept his eyes closed all the way until he felt the soft grass under his feet. Sandy was running around screaming, "Woah, woah, dude, you did it! You da *Big* Bird!" Tiago saw he was about ten metres away from the tree. He had fallen in a big arch. "You went down in slow motion. You weren't flying but you weren't falling either. You were just resisting gravity enough to not hurt yourself. I've never seen anything like this! This doesn't exist dude! You are like a unicorn – no, no, the other horse... a pegasus! That's right, you are a freaking Pegasus-Bro!"

TWENTY EIGHT

Alba

THE SEA WAS FLAT like a mirror and the boats floated silently, their crews asleep after having spent the night awake looking for the kids. Alba saw that the turtle was waiting for them in the distance and she showed it to Pedro Luis and the dogs. They began to swim following the beautiful animal and it guided them in an elaborate zig zag between the boats, as if it knew the best route to get to the boat, completely unnoticed.

Finally, after almost an hour of swimming, they reached *El Guácharo*. When she saw it, Alba couldn't help but think of *Abuela Moto* and all that she had done for her granddaughter. She was about to get on the boat when she noticed two soldiers were sleeping inside. They woke up instantly.

"Chúo. Did you hear that?" Whispered the one closest to Alba.

"Yes, be quiet," said the second, and they remained silent for what seemed like an eternity to the kids.

"Doesn't seem to be anything. What time is it?" "It's almost seven o'clock."

"Do you think they will give us breakfast today, with this search and everything?"

"I don't think so, but I bet the generals are gorging themselves on *arepas* right now."

"Oh, an arepita… I haven't eaten one in so long. The last time was the morning I joined the army. My mother got the flour from a neighbour and made me a single arepita with butter to say goodbye. I will never forget it. My little brothers watching me, I couldn't even eat it, just one bite and then I gave it to them. You know? I did this army thing for them, for my mother, so they could pay for the house and be able to stay there. They were kicking us out."

"Yes, me too. My wife is pregnant and we didn't even have enough to eat a single arepa. We only ate lentil soup so watery that we could count the lentils. They offered us an allowance for my wife and well, here I am, even though they haven't paid her in two months and I don't know what to do."

"It's not easy, my brother. But hey, we have to take it day by day. And someday things will get better…"

Alba felt remorse for all her actions on the island. She had felt so clever playing tricks on the soldiers and now she realized they were as much victims as any other Venezuelan. The generals, the politicians, the corrupt – those were the ones who had to be brought to justice.

"Well, let's hope there is coffee at least."

"Yes, but I swear, Chúo, if it's salty today, I'll swim right back to Caracas." "*Naguará!*"

The two soldiers got off the boat laughing and talking a little more animatedly, and Alba thought about what was going to happen to them and their families when they discovered that the *peñero* was missing. She tried to find some way to help them so they wouldn't be blamed, but nothing came to mind. Finally, she decided to leave the boat there and continue on swimming with the turtle. Sooner or later she would have to say goodbye to Pedro Luis and the dogs. Minus well be now. And someday, she would return to get her *peñero* back. Alba was so lost in her thoughts that she didn't notice that the others were already on the boat and that Pedro Luis was starting the engine.

"No! Pedro, don't turn it on, they'll hea…"

There was no choice; Alba had to jump into the *peñero*, pushing Pedro Luis away from the engine and giving it full throttle. Fortunately, the soldiers in the boats were slow to react. Waking up surprised by the noise, they tried to get their anchors out of the water as quickly as possible but could not make their way before *El Guácharo* was lost in the northeast corner of the island, out of sight.

Luck was on their side, the gas containers were still full, and that made it possible for Alba and her friends to continue cruising all day in a northeast direction towards Bonaire. Alba's anger with Pedro Luis did not subside until later that night when it was replaced by a feeling of anticipation for what she was about to do.

TWENTY NINE

Abuela Moto

Doña Coromoto opened her eyes. The light of the full moon was streaming in through the window and falling directly onto her face, waking her from an uneasy sleep. She turned on her bedside lamp and put her glasses on to look at the time. It was four thirty in the morning on October 28, 2015. It was the twins' birthday. She got out of bed with some effort.

She wrapped herself in her robe and left the house, walking slowly toward Alba's favorite beach. It was a wonderful night with thousands of shining stars, and a breeze as soft as a whisper. *Abuela Moto* looked up at the round, perfect moon. What a coincidence... A full moon on her grandchildren's birthday. They would be fifteen years old. If her daughter Cecilia could see them – well, feel – as *Abuela Moto* did whenever she could... She would be so proud.

After the storm, a couple of weeks ago, *Abuela Moto* started using her power to look for her grandchildren and feel their presence, and more and more she was able to sense their feelings and emotions. It was something she had never done in all her years, something she didn't know she could do. On this very special night, she closed her eyes and searched for the girl, heading northeast as always. She found her quickly. She was standing on her boat, upright, and as soon as she felt the breeze, she smiled, sure that it was her grandmother. *Doña Coromoto* trembled with that connection of love. Alba felt at peace, determined, and even enthusiastic; she was about to do something very important… then she lost her. This happened often, since it was a very difficult task for *Doña Coromoto* to use her powers in this way. Almost as difficult as getting in and out of bed.

She sat down laboriously in the sand and waited a while to recover before trying again with Tiago. She was awakened by the squawk of a seagull and realized she had fallen asleep. She looked at her watch; it was half past six in the morning. She struggled to her feet and washed her face with the seawater. Concentrating again, she passed the point where Alba was and continued on northeast looking for her grandson. She searched and searched but there was no trace of him. Until finally, on the verge of giving up, guessing that Tiago was on land, she finally saw him. He was on an island, on the edge of a cliff, about to be in the air. Perhaps that was why she was able to finally sense him. Like Alba, he was doing something monumental; he had the same feeling of anticipation. But unlike her, he was undecided, paralyzed, terrified. He looked like a little bird just before its first flight, hesitating between jumping or going back to snuggle in its nest. At that moment, *Doña Coromoto* understood everything, she understood what her grandchildren were about to do: they were going to activate their powers themselves, each without knowing the other was doing it too, each on their fifteenth birthday. Alba was ready, but Tiago was not.

Abuela Moto knew she had to help him, and with renewed effort she drew in more power than she ever had, wrapping Tiago in a soft hug and saying: "Yes Tiago, you *can* fly."

She gently pulled him by the hand and felt him step into the air. It was the last thing she saw before falling to her knees with the biggest smile ever seen on that beach. Even if she couldn't get up for hours, this would be the happiest day of her life.

THIRTY

Alba

THEY DECIDED TO ANCHOR. It was getting dark and they couldn't see well even with a full moon. They had no food, so they just sipped water and got ready for an uncomfortable sleep. Alba said goodnight to the dogs and gave Pedro Luis a quick glance before jumping in the water. She saw the head of the turtle coming up for air and wondered why she was still with them.

Alba felt calmer in the water. She had been thinking about the two soldiers she overheard that morning and the other soldiers who undoubtedly had similar stories. But now, at night, with the full moon at sea, La Orchila seemed to be in another universe. She decided to focus on her mission again. She promised herself that after finding her brother she would do something to make things better in her country, but for now, she had to honour the first promise she had made. She took out the photo she kept inside her bathing suit and looked at it for a long time. The turtle had told her that Tiago was in the Caribbean sea, searching for her. This changed everything. For now she was heading to Bonaire, but then where should she go? Where would Tiago be? Had they already passed each other? Something told her no, not yet. As well as the fact that she hadn't travelled too far these past couple of weeks; she hadn't even left Venezuelan waters.

There was a place where Tiago would surely stop by: the co-ordinates 16°46'N 76°40'W, where *Las Luces*, the sailboat that had been their home for the first seven years of their lives, lay sunken in the deep. Up until this point in her adventure, she hadn't thought about this, as she had been simply more focused on surviving. But now, it all made sense: she was always headed to 16°46'N 76°40'W, she had always had those coordinates in her subconscious and she had always known deep down that the true beginning of her journey was right there. Tiago would definitely go there.

Alba slept a few hours and just before dawn she got back into the little boat, gently waking Pedro Luis and the dogs. She had been tempted not to. It would have been easier, but she knew they wouldn't have forgiven her for leaving without saying goodbye.

"Pedro Luis, I have to tell you something.""Are we caught?"

"No, not at all, we are safe. It's something else."

· Pedro Luis got up and Pepe and Pepito stood on guard, ready for Alba's important news.

"I'm leaving Pedro. I want you to keep *El Guácharo* and return with the dogs to Margarita. Look for my grandmother, *Doña Coromoto*, in Boca de Pozo; you will all be able to live with her."

"And you?" Pedro Luis asked in surprise, thinking he must be dreaming this.

"I'll be fine, better than fine." Alba said with a genuine smile. "I have to do something that only I alone can do. I can't take anyone else... just the turtle... if you want to come," said Alba, turning to the turtle who was just coming up for air with perfect timing.

"Wait! Wait! Wait! Just a moment! Are you telling me that you are going alone? Where are you going? To the bottom of the sea?" Pedro Luis laughed, proud of his humour.

"Exactly. I'm going to swim. You can't stop me. It is something bigger than you and me. And maybe one day I'll explain it to you, but for now you have to trust me. Okay?" Alba put her hand on Pedro Luis's shoulder, a gesture that completely disarmed him.

"Okay."

"I want you to know that I do trust you, enough to send you with my dogs to live with my grandmother. Yesterday I got very angry, but it was more with myself than you. I'm sorry for not talking to you all day." Alba said, looking away. "And I also want you to know that you are nothing like Edgar." She continued without raising her gaze.

"Thank you," said Pedro Luis sadly. Then he remembered something, "I want you to wear this." He took out a large black plastic watch from his pocket. Looking at Alba's ignorant face, he explained. "It's a GPS. It measures latitude and longitude and much more. You are going to need it, your little compass is not going to be of any use to you."

"But it's yours, I can't take it away from you. You are also going to need it." Alba replied, with mixed feelings because without a doubt the GPS would be essential for her objective of reaching those very specific coordinates.

"No, it is not mine. I stole it from *General Ceballos*... and if you leave me the compass it will be more than enough to get to Margarita."

"Okay. Thanks Pedro Luis." Alba took the GPS and with the boy's help she entered the coordinates.

Alba turned and hugged Pepe and Pepito, not knowing if she'd ever see them again, and thanked them with all her heart for being her first friends on this journey. With perfect balance, she stood on the small triangle of the boat's bow and thanked the 'most beautiful *peñero* in the world.' Thinking of her *Abuela Moto*, she told her in her mind: *'I'm going to do it, grandma, I'm going to do it.'* And she felt the familiar breeze caressing her face, reminding her once again that she was not alone.

She looked once more at her friends and, finally, she said to Pedro Luis. "My name is Alba Castillo."

Then she turned towards the sea and the sun rising from the water, and she dove in.

THIRTY ONE

Tiago

"WAKE UP, LITTLE B!" Tiago opened his eyes. It was still dark, but there was a flame so close to his face that he could smell his eyebrows burning.

"Sandy? Are you trying to kill me?"

"Sorry bud, ahem..." and Sandy began to sing in the most high pitched, off-key manner possible. "Happy birthday to youuuuuuuuuu..."

Tiago smiled and remembered: it was his birthday! He had completely forgotten. They had talked about it a few days ago, but in all his emotional turmoil it had slipped his mind. He sat up and looked at a beautiful carrot cake in front of him; his favourite! He happily blew out the candle after first making his wish – that he would find his sister.

Sandy clapped and seemingly out of nowhere produced two forks and two cups of black coffee. Tiago looked at his friend with fondness. "You are my best friend. Thank you for everything you do for me. I don't take it for granted."

Sandy swallowed hard. "Thank *you* for what you do for me, bro."

They devoured the delicious cake, which Dickie made and had quietly brought to the marina the night before while Tiago was sleeping. Then Sandy got up, all business again. "Okay, now, to your birthday present. Get dressed. We have to go."

"What time is it? Where are we going this early?"

"It's 5:22am. Come on, I'll tell you on the way," answered Sandy, unceremoniously taking away Tiago's coffee.

There was an old military jeep outside the marina. It had no roof, no doors, and no roll bars. Sandy pulled the keys out of his pocket, jumped in, and started it.

Tiago didn't understand. "Is this my birthday present?" he asked.

"No, no, this swell piece of metal is a loaner from a guy I know," replied Sandy. "Get in!"

They drove a little over an hour along the east coast watching one of the most incredible sunrises either of them had ever seen. Tiago imagined flying straight over the sea, into the emerging red sun, and then melting away like Icarus. They turned inland onto a very rough road that rattled them around for another hour. Tiago noted Sandy was a conscientious driver, something he would never have guessed, but it made total sense as Sandy was also a meticulous sailor.

"Now we walk," said Sandy, parking the jeep behind some houses. They started a short trek along a beautiful river. After about five minutes, Tiago heard the rumble of water and looked up to see a big waterfall. It was more than twenty metres high and about the same width. It was man-made, and he later found out it had once been a dam. They walked closer until they were at the foot of the falls and refreshed themselves under its powerful stream.

"This is something else, Sandy. What a wonderful birthday present. Thank you." said Tiago feeling grateful.

"I'm glad you like it, but your real present is at the top. Fancy more climbing?" asked Sandy, sounding a little nervous.

They clambered up the side of the falls. It was an easy climb for Tiago, but he had to help his unsteady friend. It was very peaceful at the top where the shallow water moved ever slowly to the edge before falling, turning into thunderous rainbow-hued foam. The waterfall faced southwest, and they could see the river's path cutting through the trees on its way to the sea.

They walked along the edge of the falls, which formed a wide arch, and stopped exactly in the middle of the concave centre; the soft current scarcely put any pressure on their bare legs. Sandy turned from the view and looked at Tiago. "I'm going to go for a walk now. I thought that perhaps this view, this height, might inspire you to…"

"To what?" Asked Tiago dumbfounded, but Sandy had already started walking away. Then it hit him – Sandy was hoping it would inspire him to fly. Tiago's jaw dropped. Sandy had some real nerve. He could never… it was too open, too wide, too high…

Sandy stopped at the shore, turned back, and shouted to Tiago. "You know you won't hurt yourself. You know you can jump. But now's the time to find out if you can really soar!" And he disappeared in the bush.

True, it was a fact that Tiago had jumped from a third-story balcony, about fifteen metres high, and absolutely nothing had happened to him – not a scratch. He had jumped again yesterday, too. This was his chance to refocus and try to really fly, not just land softly. He stepped closer to the edge and made the mistake of looking down. He could see the rocks at the bottom under about one metre of water, too shallow to fall into. He recoiled, remembering the stories he had read on the internet. Why was he doubting himself now? He could do it, he knew it. He just had to trust.

Tiago looked out to the horizon and whispered, 'help me' to no one in particular. Just then a lively gust of wind hit him straight on, almost knocking him backwards, but it wrapped itself around him preventing his fall. The air current gently lifted his left hand pulling it towards the precipice. Tiago was stunned. Then he heard it clear as day, the voice of his beloved *Abuela Moto*. A thousand memories from his childhood flashed back all at once and seemed to rush straight into his heart, filling it up so much it felt as if it could burst out of his chest.

Tiago let himself be pulled off the edge. He began falling slowly just as he had done on the other occasions. Then he registered what his grandma had just said: He *could* fly, he really could. *Abuela Moto* also said Alba was in this very moment making her way to him. Alba knew he was alive, she was coming for him. He looked up at the sky and the tiny movement of his head forced his body to follow. His other arm reached forward as well and he rose up much higher than the top of the falls. He followed the course of the river until he found himself flying over the sea.

THIRTY TWO

Alba

ALBA SWAM AWAY from the boat and her friends. She already missed them. If it hadn't been for the turtle beside her she would have turned around. She noticed this time she was able to swim faster, with less effort, she was less thirsty and had no discomfort in her eyes. She had started out swimming freestyle, as she always did, but then began spending more time underwater.

After a few hours, the turtle started to descend. Alba would follow her as far as she could and then go up. The turtle would head up with her and they would take a breath together and go down again. They continued like this for a long time, going down a little deeper each time, spending more time under the water, and coming up less times to breathe.

Alba knew exactly what was happening. She could feel her sight sharpening, her body becoming more agile, and her movements more efficient. She couldn't stop smiling. She had always imagined that something dramatic would turn on her gift, like the first time when she was saved from the shipwreck. But no, all she needed to do now was to be herself. She had to heal her heart and forgive and the rest would be as easy as swimming.

Little by little, the water became clearer and Alba could see all the seabed's secrets. Fish, plants, corals, and sand became real, with all their details fully discernible. It wasn't like in an aquarium with glass enlarging them and a phosphorescent light distorting the colours. Nor like when you see through a foggy mask. In this case, the beings and formations that surrounded Alba were as obvious as the birds and insects on the shore, as the piglets and chickens in her village, as the palm trees and rocks on her island.

Alba realized she had spent a long time without going up for air, perhaps over an hour. She remembered reading about how whales can stay submerged for ninety minutes because they have proteins in their blood that fill their muscles with oxygen. Maybe she also had this same molecular structure, or maybe it was just magic.

She began to feel hungry and looked at the fish, thinking she could never catch one without a harpoon or some other instrument. Besides, the idea of eating raw fish was a little disgusting to her, except of course her grandma's delicious ceviche. Perhaps she would change her mind in the future, but for now she decided to sit on the sandy bottom holding on to a large stone, and eat the seaweed around her. As she put the first bit in her mouth, it filled with water and Alba realized with a chuckle that she couldn't yet eat under the sea.

She pulled as much algae as she could and rose to the surface, feeling an increasingly strong desire to breathe. It wasn't something sudden or exasperating, it was just her body, telling her that it was a bit fatigued and needed air to recover. When she reached the surface she took a deeper breath than she ever had before, and she looked around appreciating how bright the sky and the sun were. Floating on the surface was even easier than before and she ate her

fill, enjoying the seaweed which didn't taste bad at all. Surprised she wasn't thirsty, she thought that maybe it was because, like fish, she was able to rehydrate with the water contained in the algae.

She rested a bit, appreciating the warmth of the sun on her skin, and went down once more to continue her journey.

THIRTY THREE

Tiago

T IAGO LANDED ON A SANDY beach: he really had flown all this way! He was finally able to stop doubting and just relish in the incredibility of it all. He wondered if he could fly back and how to do it. Would he need to climb a tree and jump? Or could he just lift himself off the ground like Superman? He chuckled. He was like a comic book superhero now. It was all so very surreal. He gave it a try, jumping up and launching his arms forward, but nothing happened. Then he tried again, running along the deserted beach, he leapt into the air and it happened; he was aloft and heading upwards. He looked over at the river and immediately his body followed; wherever he looked, that's where he went.

He felt the wind and wondered if his grandmother was still with him. He glanced down and couldn't believe what was happening. He closed his eyes and focused on the sensation of flying. It felt like being underwater, similar to when he pushed off from the end of a pool and zoomed torpedo-like to the other end. But it was faster than being underwater and with less resistance. He saw the falls, and Sandy standing at the top of them in the mid-point between the two shores, where Tiago had been just a few minutes ago. Sandy was jumping and shouting wildly.

Landing was much easier than taking off. He had barely touched down when Sandy knocked him over in the water with a giant hug. He was laughing, shouting, and boisterously celebrating Tiago's success. Tiago let himself be silly too, he was unbelievably happy.

The revelry slowly died down and they caught their breath, half-floating on the shallow water. "*Una volta che abbiate conosciuto il volo, camminerete sulla terra guardando il cielo,*" quoted Sandy in perfect Italian. "Leonardo da Vinci."

"What does it mean?" Asked Tiago, recognizing the word *cielo* meaning sky in Spanish.

"Once you have known flight you will walk the earth with your eyes turned skywards," said Sandy solemnly.

"That's true," said Tiago thinking he had spent most of his life looking in one form or another up at the sky.

"Tiago, no one must know. And I mean no one!" Sandy sat up. "This is of the utmost importance buddy. Anyone finds out and you'll spend the rest of your life in labs and military compounds and you'll never look up at the sky again. You'll never be free."

"That's true too," replied Tiago, understanding the responsibility they both carried. "Sandy, I know where we should go next."

THIRTY FOUR

Alba

EACH TIME SHE WENT BACK UNDERWATER, Alba would forget a little more about the surface and her mind began to see the aquatic world as her complete reality.

"Why are you with me, turtle?" Alba asked one day, pressing her nose to the beak of the great animal.

"Because you need me," she heard in her mind.

At that moment, six gray figures heading southeast swam in front of them. They were bottlenose dolphins. Amazed, Alba moved away from the turtle towards them and in a few seconds she was among the beautiful animals.

They surrounded her, examining her with friendly curiosity and nuzzling her like in a game. Alba noticed that one of them had a plastic bag stuck to his spine; it looked like he was wearing a white scarf. Alba approached him gently and asked if she could help him.

Somehow, the dolphin understood and let her take the bag from him. Released, he gave several turns of happiness and relief and Alba was welcomed to the pack.

Alba felt a strong desire to follow them. She wasn't forgetting her mission, but she was very curious and felt a little break would do her good. She glanced at the turtle in the distance and tried to call her over, perhaps they would also accept her. But the turtle turned away. Alba then debated for a while and finally decided to stay with the pack for a short time. She set her GPS coordinates to know where to return, and hoped with all her heart that the turtle was waiting for her when she came back.

It's difficult to know how long she was with the dolphins. It was more than a couple of days. Maybe a week, or two? With every minute that passed, Alba's mind failed to recall who she had been on the surface and she even began to forget about her brother, her grandmother, and her mission.

Every day the girl became more like the cetaceans. She could swim as fast as they could and now she could eat the fish they caught underwater, without a problem. She also became able to communicate with them. At first she did it in a very basic way, trying to imitate their clicks, but soon she learned the whistle or proper name for each one of them, and then she began to understand commands such as 'let's hunt' or 'attention, danger.'

There was the lead dolphin, a pair of males, and two mothers with their respective babies. Looking at them, Alba realized more and more that these amazing animals had evolved specifically to survive in this environment and that therefore it was unequivocally pure magic what made her survive under the sea.

One of the mothers took a special interest in Alba, teaching her how to catch large fish and how to look for smaller ones under the sand. To do this, the dolphins first found sponges and placed them on their snouts to protect them from rocks and corals. The mother brought over two sponges to Alba knowing that she would use her hands and not her mouth. After some time, Alba learned a new click from the pack: her own name! Filled with admiration and love for these animals, the idea of returning to the world to which she once belonged became increasingly difficult.

One afternoon as the adults hunted, Alba frolicked with the babies. They would make large air rings out of their nostrils and she would try to go through without breaking them. Suddenly, the water was filled with hundreds of transparent balloons with long tentacles. The babies, with their thick skins resistant to stings, began to hunt the jellyfish very carefully, eating the heads. But more and more came and the little dolphins ingeniously began to rise to the surface bouncing off the bells of the jellyfish.

Alba tried to do the same but she was not as agile as the dolphins and soon enough she was stung by the tentacles. Feeling an electrical pain in her leg, Alba tried to get to the surface, kicking hard at the jellyfish. But all her strength and determination were not enough, and time and time again she was stung by the poisonous invertebrates. Her whole body began burning in agony and she could no longer swim, her only option was to drop to the bottom of the sea under the jellies. So she emptied her lungs and let herself sink. Once on the sand, she huddled around a large stone and sank again, this time into a fiery pit of delirium.

After a while, she felt two large smooth, rubbery bodies under her arms slowly propelling her upward. Her empty lungs buckled as she ascended until she broke the water barrier and felt the dry heat of the sun on her bruised face. She sucked in the air as the two dolphins swam slowly and gently together to keep her perfectly supported. Little by little she came to a slow breathing rhythm and was able to assess the damage on her body. Her arms, legs, neck, and face resembled a map of ocean currents she had once seen at school, severely marked by the long tentacles. Every laceration felt raw. She also felt pain in her chest and a terrible headache. Alba felt defeated and, although she appreciated the dolphins' help, a part of her wished they had left her alone at the bottom of the sea.

Suddenly, she spotted the head of the great turtle a few feet away. Puffing through her nose, she approached Alba and the dolphins. The turtle *had* followed her! Any thought of getting lost on the ocean floor rushed out of Alba's mind. She slowly let go of the dolphins and thanked them with a short click. She swam with difficulty towards the turtle and when they reached each other they touched their noses.

"I'm so sorry. Please take me to Tiago." The turtle nodded and let Alba slowly climb onto her great shell.

The other dolphins appeared on the surface knowing that it was time for Alba to leave them. They swam around her in a circle, jumping high and clicking Alba's name in unison. Alba noticed they seemed to be taking them in a specific direction and, after a while, they felt a strong warm current pulling them in a northwesterly direction. Later Alba would discover the dolphins had left them in the Caribbean Current, the fastest way to get to 16°46'N 76°40'W.

The cetaceans stayed with them for a while and then, one by one, they drifted away from the current. Alba's tears disappeared into the sea. She felt true love and gratitude for these creatures who

displayed a purer and nobler spirit than almost any of the humans she knew.

Once they were left alone in the stream, Alba fell asleep soundly. She could finally rest because she was back on the right path to her brother.

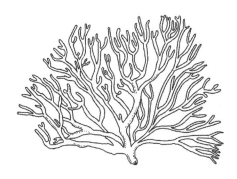

THIRTY FIVE

Tiago

"SIXTEEN, FORTY-SIX NORTH, seventy-six, forty west," said Tiago.

"Okay," answered Sandy, finding it on the map. "It's close enough to shore so we'll be able to run back and forth for supplies and refill our air tanks." They had decided that when they arrived at the coordinates, instead of idly waiting for Alba, they would dive the site in the hopes of finding the sunken sailboat. "It's deep bud, depending on where the boat is, we are looking at a forty to fifty metre dive. Have you been that deep before?"

"No, never past thirty," replied Tiago thinking he might be in way over his head.

"It's okay, we'll do a few prep dives, and I'll have your back," Sandy assured him. As with everything sea-related, Sandy was an expert. He was a certified technical scuba diver and had been a diving instructor back in Key West.

They sailed for a few hours with favourable winds and a cloudless sky, starting before dawn so that Tiago could fly and follow *Hope* without fear of being seen. As soon as they arrived at the coordinates, around noon, Tiago felt like a crater would open up under him and swallow him whole into its darkness. Somewhere under them laid the remains of his childhood home. What had been the most solid and real thing in his life rested broken and forgotten at the bottom of the sea.

It was time to get ready for a practice dive. They had filled all their scuba tanks at a dive shop in Port Royal and let them know where they'd be in case of an emergency. Sandy programmed his computer for a thirty metre dive. They slipped into the water, oriented themselves, and began their slow descent, equalizing every half metre down or so.

Being so deep underwater was such a strange experience for Tiago. He felt restricted and uncomfortable. In the air he could go as fast and as high as he dared without any consequences; up there he was untouchable. Down in the deep blue he was subjected to the rules of pressure and decompression, he was weighed down by twin diving tanks, and had a giant regulator in his mouth reminding him he really did not belong under the sea. Gauging their descent carefully, they reached their depth and spent ten minutes at thirty metres before slowly ascending. The sea was vast and dark blue, and as far from the shore as they were, it was a rather lonely place.

They spent the next three days diving in the mornings, fishing in the afternoons, and grilling their catch in the evenings. With each dive they went deeper, and soon they were methodically exploring the sea bottom in a carefully mapped trajectory that would ensure they covered the most amount of ground around the coordinates.

"You really think she's going to come?" Sandy asked one night.

"Yeah, but I don't know when, that's the thing. I do know she's going to be here at some point. I know it like I know I can fly."

Tiago answered.

"Well, that's good enough for me," replied his friend. "In the meantime, we'll keep at it. Tomorrow is our second-to-last quadrant. Let's see if we can find your home."

The next morning they prepared their gear. They had returned to Port Royal a few times to refill their tanks. At this depth, they spent most of their air on the descent and ascent, leaving them very little time at the bottom of the sea. There were two reasons for this: the first being that at greater depths the body consumes oxygen much faster than higher up, and the second was that they needed to ascend very slowly and stop at certain points in order to decompress properly.

Tiago felt nervous every time they went down to such great depths, but he was eager to have the opportunity to find *Las Luces*. Since the storm eight years ago, he had wanted nothing more than to return to the site. And here he was now having almost drowned, discovering that he could fly, and finding out that his sister was alive and on her way to him.

All was good upon descent and he smiled as he always did when they reached the bottom, picking up sand and letting it run through his fingers. Sandy marked their coordinates in his dive computer and then began leading them against the current in what was meant to be a large circle. But before they got far, luck finally struck and there she was, *Las Luces*.

Tiago was surprised by how shiny the boat was. It looked almost new with its perfect white hull. Seeing the broken mast brought back the memory of having perched on it for so long: cold, afraid, and so very alone. He knew they didn't have much time, so he began swimming toward the boat until a shadow to the side distracted him. He looked over with wonder and then love filled his eyes. It was his mother.

"Mami?"

"Tiago, my baby. Yes, it's me." Speaking in Spanish. She wore her black diving suit but no diving gear and was perfectly at ease underwater, unaffected by the pressure or the lack of air. Tiago swam toward her. *"Tiaguito, no. Stop. You can't follow me. Listen carefully: I had to do it. I had to do it for the two of you, so you could save yourselves. Remember this, Tiago. And remember that I love you from the bottom of the sea…"*

She swam away with incredible speed and Tiago tried to follow her, but he felt the restraint of two strong arms around him. He fought frantically to free himself so he could follow her. He fought and fought until he blacked out.

When he awoke, he was back on the boat.

"Dude, you gave me another scare," sighed Sandy looking exhausted after hoisting his friend up for almost fifty metres. "You got narced man!" He was referring to narcosis, the physical and mental impairment divers can experience at greater depths because of the anesthetic effect of nitrogen and other gases on the brain. "You swam away and I had to hold you from going off into a cliff. With your weights you would have gone straight down, bud. It was very scary. You fought me off fiercely and then you passed out. I knew you were just narced, but it was still really bad."

"I'm so sorry, Sandy," answered Tiago, he couldn't remember anything. Only the image of beautiful *Las Luces* at the bottom of the sea.

"It's okay, bro," Sandy hesitated. "Listen, we've located the boat. Isn't that great?" He patted Tiago's shoulder. "I think we should go to shore and regroup, and then we can come back. Maybe Alba isn't coming just yet..."

Tiago had an uneasy sleep that night. He dreamt he was underwater, dizzy and disoriented. He was going down, down, down, without ever hitting bottom. He woke up, calmed himself and fell asleep, but the dream started all over again. He woke a second time, and went up on deck. The giant waning moon illuminated the calm surface of the water with its iridescent white light. It made the sea look like a massive cake covered in glittering sugar icing.

Looking at the moon, he asked himself what was he supposed to do now, and what did all of this mean. Once again he was certain of nothing, he had to let go, wait it out, and trust in the wind that kept whispering to him. He took a breath and lifted off - only flying would ease his mind.

THIRTY SIX

Alba

ALBA OPENED HER EYES and found they were no longer moving at high speed, they had left the current. Her head didn't hurt anymore and she felt a little less pain from her injuries. She dismounted the turtle and began to swim on her own. The sea seemed bigger here, vaster. It was much deeper than before and Alba couldn't see the bottom. For the first time, she was a little afraid underwater and wanted to rise to the surface. She looked at her GPS and realized that she had reached her destination. A different kind of fear gripped her.

Still, she turned, looking around for the sailboat, and quickly realized that she would have to go down into the dark. She felt like throwing up, this was too much for her. Abandoned at sea by pirates, pursued on land by the military, stung underwater by dozens of jellyfish... None of it added up to what she had to face now. She had dreamed of returning to the shipwreck site but never imagined she would actually have a chance to find the ship and possibly explore it. Now, thanks to her gift, she had an obligation to look for it, there was no other option. It was the hardest thing she had ever done.

She calmed herself down and grabbed onto the shell of the turtle, who in turn, understood everything and began to descend slowly and deliberately. Alba thought about the pressure and began equalizing her ears just in case, but she stopped when she noticed it didn't really make any difference.

Alba could feel the changes with every meter they descended, she was getting colder and colder and her body was contracting. She began to shake, and after a while the GPS' glass shattered with a furious crack. At last she saw the bottom, in grayish tones from the lack of light. The turtle began to swim in larger and larger circles, tracking the sand. Alba imagined that depending on the wind and current when it sank, the sailboat could be as much as one to a hundred kilometers from the coordinates. They would need luck to find it, since Alba didn't know how much longer she could stay at this depth.

Little by little her eyes began to adapt to the opacity and her body grew warmer. She picked up a large stone and released the turtle, walking beside her on the cold sand. Alba felt her gift kick into a higher gear and wondered how the magic inside her could defy so many laws of physics. Lost in thought, she almost bumped into a large formation and she immediately understood that it was *Las Luces*.

Alba sat on the bottom of the sea with her rock, as she had done so many times, and began to cry. After a long time she calmed down, deciding to save her emotions for later and focus on examining the ship.

Las Luces looked almost as good as it had before. The white of her hull shone brighter than in the sun and although she was full of shells and ballads, she looked like she had sunk just a couple of months ago, and not eight years. She was leaning on her side, at an angle on her keel, as if she had been gently placed on the sand instead of having fallen nearly fifty meters. Her only imperfection was the broken mast.

Alba walked over and clung to a railing, leaving the stone on the sand. She had to work hard not to be pulled up. Being less dense than water seemed to be the only physical limitation that her gift could not overcome. She was in the stern, she grabbed the wheel and lost herself in the memory of those warm days when she was sailing with her family. There was always so much noise on the boat: laughter, screams, silly fights between her and her brother, music, creaking wood, and the wind, always the wind. And now the ship was completely silent. She kept exploring the deck, remembering little details. She found the two ropes with which they practiced their knots and tied them around her waist.

She went below-deck, where it was much darker, but Alba knew her way around. Plates, cutlery, cushions, and a thousand other things covered the floor and other surfaces. With her back against the ceiling, she ran her hands along the small galley (kitchen); the desk where the radio, the GPS, and all the records were; and the saloon (living room), with a folding dining table. Then she headed aft, recognizing the tiny head (bathroom), her cabin with her and Tiago's bunk beds, and finally her mother's.

Although the cabin was messy and shrouded in darkness, Alba felt completely comfortable inside it, after all, this had been her home since she was born until she went to live with her grandmother. She remembered where the diving equipment was and found her mother's weight harness, which now fit her perfectly. She also found a diving light that miraculously still worked. With this bit of light, Alba proceeded to put everything in its place as best as she could. She put away all the floating objects such as papers and bags and, after a while everything looked impeccable. She even considered staying there for a while, but knew that sooner or later the depth would affect her, even with her gift.

Interestingly, she did not feel as sad as when she first discovered the boat. On the contrary, she thought about how lucky she was to have such an amazing mother and such an adventurous childhood. From now on, this place would no longer be one of fear and sadness, but one of commemoration. She wished, with all her heart, that she could soon tell her brother about this experience and she felt anxious to go up and continue with her mission. But she remembered something first: there was a yellow plastic box with an airtight seal in which her mother kept all the important documents in water-proof bags.

Alba looked for it and there it was, in its place. She almost opened it knowing that it was most likely already full of water, but then realized right away that this was something she had to do with Tiago.

At last she was ready to go up to the surface. She looked around one last time and thanked the sailboat. She left the light on and went out to meet the turtle. She dropped one of the weights and held onto the turtle's shell with one hand while holding the yellow box with the other, tying it with the ropes just in case. She relied on the turtle's ability to ascend more slowly than her, and thus avoid any possible complications of a rapid ascent. The turtle did take much longer to go up than it had to descend. Every so often, Alba would drop off another weight, always staring at the bright light that remained at the bottom of the sea.

Finally, Alba looked up and around; she felt flooded with light. They were about six meters from the surface and the turtle stopped ascending. Alba looked up, the brightness was overwhelming, but it wasn't daytime. A large moon was visible through the water and in its shadow there was the hull of a sailboat.

THIRTY SEVEN

Alba & Tiago

ALBA ROSE CAUTIOUSLY TO THE SURFACE and took a deep breath, delighted to feel the warm and dry air welcoming her. She looked at the sky, the moon, and the stars, and it occurred to her that the sky was like an infinite sea. She saw a shadow above her, moving in great circles around the sailboat. It looked like a giant bird.

Suddenly, the figure stopped in midair and looked into her eyes. It was not a bird, it was Tiago, her brother. There was no doubt. The boy descended until he landed on the sailboat.

"Alba! Alba! Is that you?" Tiago yelled, his voice torn with emotion.

"Tiago..." Alba murmured, unable to speak any louder after having been so long under water.

Tiago threw himself into the sea and swam frantically towards his sister, who floated effortlessly in the cold water. He stopped just about a meter away from her and looked at her slowly. Without a doubt, it was Alba, but at the same time it was not her. The girl in front of him was complete wilderness, she looked more like a sea creature than a human. Her hair was like a bundle of seaweed and her skin was striped like that of a cardinal fish. And what struck Tiago the most were her eyes, which had a silver glassy quality, as if they belonged to a being from the deep.

Alba, studying her brother with her eyes that were just beginning to adjust to the surface, noticed that Tiago was an extended version of the seven-year-old Tiago she remembered. He was taller and wider, but otherwise he had the same golden hair, dark complexion, and that big smile which now seemed to sparkle like the sea. Although Alba was filled with happiness, she couldn't shake the mistrust she felt after seeing him in the air.

"You were flying…" She finally found her voice.

"Yes, it's a long story, Albita," Tiago answered without breaking his smile. "And you, where did you come from?"

Alba realized that she too had come to this meeting in a peculiar way, and it finally dawned on her that Tiago was also Mareno. She shook off the fear and pounced on her brother with a hug that almost drowned him.

Tiago was so happy, he didn't mind swallowing water. Splashing, babbling, and breathing when he could, he continued to hug his sister in the sea and guide her toward the sailboat. They got on board and looked at each other for a long time. They held hands, laughed, and hugged each other again and again. All the sadness of those eight years, all the loneliness, all the anger and anxiety, faded into thin wisps of air that dispersed into nothingness. Each one of them felt lighter, stronger, and more complete. And at that moment, Alba and Tiago felt invincible, because they had regained their other half.

They spent the next few hours telling each other all about their respective lives since the shipwreck and, in particular, talking about their last month of adventures, up until reaching *Las Luces*, which they had now both seen beneath them. Each one of them had to answer dozens of questions about their gift and perform almost as many demonstrations. They talked about Marenos and Alba told Tiago everything she knew, finally providing him the answers he so needed.

It was almost dawn when Alba quietly said to her brother.

"Tiago, do you remember what I told you, that *mami* could control the sea? Isn't it strange that she drowned in the storm? When she could have saved herself..."

"I hadn't thought about it to tell you the truth. I think I'm still processing everything," Tiago replied, a bit taken aback.

"Sometimes I think she just gave up, that she couldn't take it anymore and let herself drown," Alba confessed sadly. "That she didn't care enough about us..." She stopped speaking, realizing that even though she had forgiven her mother she had never expressed the abandonment she felt.

"No, I don't think so, Alba. There must be some explanation," said Tiago, trying to remember something.

At that moment, they heard a snort in the water, Alba's expression changed and she jumped happily into the sea. Tiago, confused, threw himself behind his sister and used all his strength to reach her. He saw Alba underwater with a beautiful turtle. The two of them rose to the surface and Alba told Tiago that the turtle was her friend and had been helping her since escaping La Orchila. She went on to explain that they could communicate if they put their faces together and that at this moment, the turtle wanted to say something to both of them. Alba held out her hand to Tiago and brought her nose close to the beak of the animal.

Tiago felt a thought form in his mind. It was not a voice but a knowledge that was grounded in his heart. These were the words of the turtle:

"Now that the two of you are together, I have something import-ant to tell you. I was here. A long time ago; the night of the storm. Back then I was a normal turtle worried only about my survival. I was surprised by the storm just like you, and saw the sailboat and your mother doing her best to navigate through the hurricane. Suddenly she jumped into the sea near me and I felt a current pulling me towards her. She kept me by her side, while she moved her hands and tried with her mind to defeat the hurricane. I understood that she was protecting me and that she could control the water. She fought for a long time with all her strength to calm the waves, but little by little she began losing the battle.

"You were both calling her from the boat and I thought she would finally get back on it, but she made one last effort and turned to me. Her eyes told me not to be afraid and I let myself be touched by her. At that moment, with her hands on my head, I felt like she was filling me with energy, purpose, and awareness. She told me: "My children are on that boat; they are my reason for being. Their only hope of survival is for me to die. My children have a gift, an ability that will save them. But that gift is asleep, it will only wake for sure when my children feel the pain of my death. What

I must do is a terrible thing, but it is the only way I can guarantee that their gift will be switched on. And I do so happily, knowing that I will save their precious lives. Turtle, I need you to watch over my children in my absence. Take care of them until they are safe. I give you all my being, so that you can guide and accompany them." Without saying more, she sank, and I never saw her again.

"I looked towards the boat and found you two clinging to each other. You had seen everything without understanding a thing. Alba, you got away from your brother and jumped into the water, taking off your life jacket so you could dive to save your mother. I tried to follow you Alba, I swear, but I couldn't. A wave swallowed you and I didn't see you again until a couple of weeks ago. I returned to the sailboat to look for you Tiago, you were alone and confused, not knowing what to do. Lightning struck the mast, splitting the wood in two, and at the same time, with the electric shock, you fell into the water. At last I was able to react in time and I caught up with you. You were unconscious on my shell the rest of the night.

"I don't know how but we were saved, the storm passed and the sun came out in the morning. Tiago, you woke up with all the sadness in the world inside of you. You saw the mast, and you simply jumped off my shell with your arms extended, and you flew towards it. Just like that. You stayed there perched like a bird for many days while the boat slowly sank. I stayed close to you until some ships came and took you away. By then, only the tip of the mast, with you on it, was left out of the water.

"Since then, I have continued to live my years slowly forgetting what happened and going back to being the turtle I once was.

Until one night a few weeks ago two sharks attacked me and some humans on a boat helped me. In the middle of the fight I went up to breathe and I saw you Tiago, and with each breath, the memory of years ago returned stronger than ever. Almost at the end, when I was sure that the other human and I were going to be eaten, you saved us.

"*Since the storm, I haven't had this level of consciousness as I have today; I think it's because we are back here in the same place where everything happened. But even at my most basic self, I knew that I had to fulfill the task your mother had given me. Tiago, I followed you for a long time, but when you arrived in a human town and stayed there for several days, I decided to continue south. And there, by luck or destiny, I found Alba.*"

At the end of the turtle's story, Tiago finally remembered what he had forgotten: his mother, fifty meters under, telling him: *'I had to do it. I had to do it for the two of you, so that you could save yourselves. Remember this, Tiago.'*

Not knowing what to say, Alba kissed the turtle in gratitude and guided Tiago, still in shock, towards the sailboat. Once on it, Alba turned to him. "Are you okay Tiaguito?"

"*Mami* always told us that she loved us from the bottom of the sea..." Tiago answered, his voice far away.

"I had forgotten, you're right. She always did say that," Alba said sadly, feeling an infinite love for her family.

THIRTY EIGHT

New Mission

THE NEXT MORNING, TIAGO PREPARED a simple breakfast of cereal, fruit, and yogurt that Alba found to be the most exquisite delicacy after weeks of eating raw fish and seaweed.

At last, Sandy came out of the cabin. Perhaps he had slept soundly without hearing any of the commotion the night before or perhaps he had decided to give the siblings some solid time alone. With Sandy, you never knew. He walked straight to Alba and held out his hand.

"It's an honor to meet you Alba," he said in perfect Spanish. "I'm Sandy. Sandy Shores with S." using the same musical intonation as he did in English.

"Just how many languages do you know?" Tiago asked him, now wondering in which language they should be speaking in. Sandy winked at him and sat down to chat with the girl.

Alba and Tiago never spoke of the turtle's words. There was nothing to say. They both understood their mother's sacrifice was a bittersweet gift that brought with it the great responsibility of living extraordinary, generous, and happy lives, at all cost.

They explained everything to Sandy, who asked to meet the turtle with whom he had fought the sharks. It was a magical encounter that neither Sandy nor the turtle would ever forget. Alba and Tiago could not get over their amazement that thanks to Sandy, and the sixth sense that he seemed to possess, this magical turtle had been able to find them.

Alba remembered the yellow box and showed it to the others. They opened it very carefully, letting the water drain out. Meticulously stored inside airtight bags were their Venezuelan passports, birth certificates, some drawings, and several old letters. They were just a little damp. At the bottom of the box there were a number of documents related to the *Trouvadore* research. Essays, photocopies of very old records, handwritten notes, emails and letters exchanged with museums and scientific research centers.

"Amazing! Your mother had evidence that there were Marenos from Cape Verde on that ship!" Sandy said, almost shouting with excitement, and then in a more somber tone. "They were kidnapped by slave hunters and forced into that galleon."

"What Mom wanted to know was if any Mareno survived the shipwreck and ended up living in Turks and Caicos," Tiago completed.

"Of course they survived," exclaimed Alba.

At that moment they heard the noise of an engine from the southeast. They turned around and saw a brown peñero with a kid and two dogs on board.

"Pedro Luis?" Alba exclaimed and immediately jumped head first into the sea. "She does this a lot," Tiago said to a gaping Sandy.

They saw how Alba swam towards the *peñero* at an amazing speed, getting on it before the boy could turn off the engine. Alba hugged the two dogs tightly and then stood in front of Pedro Luis, who sat down like a child in trouble. Towering over him, Alba gave him a scolding that lasted a while.

At last they arrived at the sailboat, tied up the boat, and came on board. Alba introduced them to Pedro Luis and Pepe and Pepito. Sandy declared it was time for a celebration and instantly produced music, soda, and many bags of chips.

Pedro Luis explained to them that as soon as he said goodbye to Alba nine days ago, he felt a knot in his chest. The dogs wouldn't stop howling on their way to Margarita, until they finally turned around remembering the coordinates Alba had programmed into the GPS. After a few adventures they happily arrived at the co-ordinates, safe and sound, and only a little hungry, which prompted Sandy to begin grilling some fish.

After a few hours Alba finally stopped looking at Pedro Luis with a scowl and told him that she was very happy to see them again. Sitting next to her brother, with the dogs at her feet, she confessed to Pedro Luis the reason she had been so angry was because she wanted *Abuela Moto* to have some company and to hear proper news from her. She had just finished saying this when a light breeze from the southeast enveloped her and Tiago in a big hug, and a whisper said to them: *'I'm not alone. My grandchildren are together and I will always be with them. I am the happiest grandmother in the world!'*

They laughed, played, swam, ate, and had fun like never before. In the evening, with the sound of the dogs' soft snoring and the oc-casional snorting from the turtle who was still with them, the four friends spoke of the future.

"And now? What is our next move?" asked Sandy mischievously.

"I will join in as long as it takes me far away from Edgar," Pedro Luis replied.

"It's obvious what we have to do," Alba said. "We have to go to *Trouvadore* and we have to find out if there are Marenos in Turks and Caicos."

"We'll do it. I'll go wherever you go, Alba," replied Tiago. And then he whispered. "Always."

TIMELINE OF EVENTS

Year 2015

Sept 3	Alba and Tiago find out about each other
Oct 15	Tiago leaves from South Palm Beach, Florida
	Alba leaves from Boca de Pozo, Margarita
	Alba spends the night in La Tortuga, Venezuela
Oct 16	Alba is left in the sea by pirates
Oct 17	Tiago is sand-barred in Ship Channel Cay, The Bahamas
	Alba arrives in La Orchila, Venezuela
Oct 22	Tiago helps Sandy fight off the sharks east of Santiago, Cuba
Oct 23	Tiago arrives in Port Antonio, Jamaica
Oct 27	Alba leaves La Orchila, Venezuela
Oct 28	Alba and Tiago's Birthdays
Oct 30	Tiago leaves Port Antonio, Jamaica
Oct 31	Tiago arrives at coordinates
Nov 7	Alba arrives at coordinates

Manufactured by Amazon.ca
Bolton, ON

29152012R00085